MW01168816

When Love Hurts

When Love Hurts

Vicki Tolver

AuthorHouse™
1663 Liberty Drive
Bloomington, IN 47403
www.authorhouse.com
Phone: 1-800-839-8640

© 2013 by Vicki Tolver. All rights reserved.

No part of this book may be reproduced, stored in a retrieval system, or transmitted by any means without the written permission of the author.

Published by AuthorHouse 03/20/2013

ISBN: 978-1-4817-2817-1 (sc)
ISBN: 978-1-4817-2816-4 (e)

Library of Congress Control Number: 2013904470

Any people depicted in stock imagery provided by Thinkstock are models, and such images are being used for illustrative purposes only.
Certain stock imagery © Thinkstock.

This book is printed on acid-free paper.

Because of the dynamic nature of the Internet, any web addresses or links contained in this book may have changed since publication and may no longer be valid. The views expressed in this work are solely those of the author and do not necessarily reflect the views of the publisher, and the publisher hereby disclaims any responsibility for them.

CONTENTS

CHAPTER 1

As I sit here staring out the window, my mind goes back to the first day we met. I thought this man was too good to be true, and guess what, he was. I think about how hot he made me. I could feel my pussy getting all wet just thinking about the hard core sex that we had. He came into my life during a very dark time. When I met him, there was a chill in my spine. Not knowing the chill would come at a price and last as long as it did. He was tall, dark and sexy. His lips so full of lust and love. His hands so soft and strong his body to die for and he dressed the part. His voice could make you melt with just a whisper. I met this stranger while trying to figure out this dark hole I was in, not knowing when I came out of that hole that he would be the one to put me back in it and some. One day while sitting in the park crying my eyes out, this shadow of a man was standing over me, I looked up in amazement as to what I saw. He asked me did I want any company and of course I said yes, wiping the tears from my eyes I can feel him staring at me, his look even made me feel hot. "Mrs. are you alright", he asked me. I couldn't help but notice how upset you are. Yes, I'm fine, thank you. Is there anything I can do to help? No, but thank you I will be fine. He continued to sit there with me and we talked as to what it seems like forever. It was time for me to head home. Thank you sir for talking to me I really do feel better. To make sure I would like to follow you home just to make sure you're safe if it's alright with you. I don't know if that's a good idea I don't even know you, well my name is Alex Nesbit and it's really nice to meet you Mrs . . . . I'm sorry Mrs. Taylor is my name and it's really nice to meet you as well. He seem like he was really nice so I thought it would be ok if he followed me home, after all I was packing a nice 380 under my clothes. I guess it shouldn't hurt if you follow me home since you've stayed out here with me on this park bench the past few hours and besides if you try anything I would just shoot you. We both started to laugh and began walking to our cars. Mr. Nesbit thank you for making me feel better, you are so welcome Mrs. Taylor, it has really been a pleasure talking with you and actually you made me feel better as well, I didn't know anything was wrong with you as good as you look. Because I look good, doesn't mean I don't have any problems. He says you are right I apologize. There is no need for apologies you didn't do anything wrong. I reached my car and he opens my door for me. Then he went to his car. I was driving an older model Taurus and of course he was driving a really nice BMW. When we reached my apartment, I parked the car and walked over to his car, thank you Mr. Nesbit for following me home I guess I'll see you at the park on our favorite bench. Thank you Mrs. Taylor and yes you will be seeing me again. I walked into my cold lonely apartment and headed straight for the bathroom to take a shower, a cold shower that is. By the time I finished lotioning my body and putting on something to sleep in, I heard a knock at my door. Who is it? It's me. I knew that voice as soon as I heard it. I opened the door and yes it was him standing there in a three piece black Armani suit, with a white shirt with white beautiful teeth to match. He had on a black tie and black shoes and oh boy he was looking good. I wanted him now. I was standing there in a silk teddy feeling refresh and lusting after him. He took my hand and led me to the couch without saying a word. His lips grasp my face and I was in heaven they were so soft and sweet than I tasted him awwwww he tasted so sweet his lips made me tingle all over, my pussy was wet and I was feeling nasty. He fingers began to glide over my nipples making them stand at attention. I started to undress him, removing his tie than unfasten his shirt all while he's kissing me. I started to shiver with lust. He kissed me harder I was panting like a puppy. His tongue moving around my nipples with such force, by now my pussy is dripping wet. I can feel mu juices flowing down my legs, as he moved down to the floor on his knees, his lips and tongue followed, he licked my body down to my pussy where I wanted him to be. He spreaded my legs and he began to lick my hot pussy his teeth griped my clitoris and he began sucking. I wanted to squirt all over his face but I had control at least for a moment. His tongue wouldn't stop the torture of my pussy I moaned so loudly I thought the world heard me scream. I was so captivated by him. His tongue thrust harder and harder and each time I screamed. I came so hard into his face it was like a waterfall, he still kept going and going finally he began to stand up. I unzipped his pants and they drop to the floor. I began to touch him softly with my lips; I can feel his erection budging out his underwear. I pulled down his boxer and began to fill my mouth with him. He smelled so good I began sucking his erect penis and listen to him moan. He grab the back of my head and thrust into my mouth until he was in the back of my throat, in and out with each thrust a louder more manly moan came out his mouth. I sucked him until he came all over my face. He pulled me up and began sucking my tongue. He grabbed my hands and led me to my bedroom. He laid me down and climb on top of me kissing me and sucking me and all I could think of was who was he and where did he come from. Was he sent just for me or was I dreaming. He glided into me and at first it was so sensual and hot. But then it got rough he fucked my pussy so hard but it felt so good and I wanted more, I didn't want him to stop I haven't felt like this before. I was hungry and it was just for him. We fucked like rabbits, by the time he was finish I fell asleep in his arms, by morning when I awoke he was gone. I was alone again, there was a note by my bedside on the night stand which said, thanks for a great evening. Dam did he just make me feel like a prostitute or what!

CHAPTER 2

I thought about him the whole day wondering if I would see him again. I didn't have his number and he didn't have mine. I thought it was a one night affair. I felt good and sad at the same time. You see I was going through a separation at the time, my husband had hurt me so bad I didn't feel sexy or worthy of a man especially this man who walked in and out of my life in one night. I am a 43 year old woman who was not like those sexy skinny girls. I was not fat but I was not small like men want their women to be. I had a fairly decent job at that time; my kids were off with their own lives. They are both married so I really felt alone. My husband wasn't happy with me he wanted someone younger and smaller and it wasn't me. He made me feel less than a woman. He would say the most horrible things to me. I thought no man would ever want me again he had my self-esteem low until I felt like a nothing. I guess that was his way of justifying what he was doing and that it was ok for him but not okay with me. I thought I was fat and ugly because he made me feel that way. All I knew was to work, come home clean and cook and serve my husband. That's the way I was brought up, to take care of home and everyone in it. I thought our sex life was good but I guess I was the only person who did. I knew something was wrong in my marriage when he stared hanging with these young skinny girls and always had somewhere to go but work. One day I came home from work early and found him in bed with this bitch that I knew. She spent a lot of time with the family until we all treated her as our family. I just snapped when I saw them in my bed. It took everything in me not to kill both of them so I moved out of my house. As time went on I wouldn't date anyone I trusted no man at all. I always thought I was fat and not sexy and all men wanted one thing "pussy". So I decided that if men can fuck around so can I. I began to satisfy myself. I explored every inch of my body and knew it better than any man could ever know. I went to the novelty store and bought all kinds of goodies. If it needed batteries I bought it from whips, handcuffs, creams and lotions. Big vibrators, small vibrators, massagers anything that will make me have multiple orgasm's. Anything to fuck any man brains out and to make me happy. I went to the strip clubs on weekends to see who I can bring home for the evening and who spending money to see pussy and ass. I took home young, old, black, white and Italian men and sometimes even women. I found myself drifting deeper and deeper into this black hole of my life and getting more dangerous with my body. I was treating my body like a prostitute. I kept the motto "you got to pay to play". But I changed all that and decided a man had to really deserve fucking me and being with me so I stopped fucking around and got myself together. I went to the park every day after work to keep from going home to my empty apartment and started writing in a journal not knowing I was being watched by this tall dark handsome guy. I met Alex in the park that cold rainy day and his touch of my hand sent chills down my spine. We spent many days and nights together. He would come to see me for lunch; sometimes we would go to his favorite hotel where he would have roses and champagne. I started making sure that every day my bra and panties match and that they were always sexy. He had a way of making me feel like the sexiest person in the world. One day I went to the hotel to see Alex for lunch. I was feeling really frisky that day and every time I thought about him I would wet my panties. I would have to sit with my legs closed most of the time when he was on my mind. Whenever I would hear his deep sexy voice my nipples would stand at attention. But anyway I walked into the room and there was a big bouquet of roses on the table. We sat down on the couch in our hotel suite. Alex poured us some champagne. We talked for a while the next thing I knew his soft hand was rubbing my legs giving me a thrill. His lips touched my neck and the sweet smell of his cologne had me melting on the couch. He slowly started to undress me and kiss me at the same time. He made me feel so good. He took off my shoes and began sucking my toes. He began moving up my thighs with his tongue kissing every inch of my legs and thighs. When arrived at my sweet candy box he began working his tongue like he was unwrapping a piece of candy. His tongue was so strong he can work a clitoris. He licked and sucked my pussy so good until I came three times back-to-back in his face. I was drained didn't know how much more I could take. He had a way of making me cum a lot before he was done with me. He moved his soft silky lips up my stomach and with his teeth he grabs my nipples. I was so turned on by now. He sucked my nipples and slid his fingers into my panties until his fingers were inside me; he began to finger fuck me while his teeth were biting my nipples. "Alex I'm cumin, I can't hold it", he said hold on baby. He slid his erect penis into my vagina and he rocked my world. His kisses are so sweet he started with such passion than it became rough and rougher like I'm the only girl to ever kiss him. He started kissing my neck my face even my eyes. By the time he got to my ears I was about to bust. Fuck me Alex please I'm so hot for you right now. He took me and rolled me on top of him. I rode that dick like I was the cowgirl and he was the horse. I straddled myself across him I went up and down twisting and turning. It felt so dam good. By then he flipped me over on my knees and got behind me and he thrust and thrust me until I thought my insides was going to come through my head. He held on to my hair and fucked me hard. Once he was done we just laid there in bed breathing hard. Let's go take a shower baby. He was standing there washing his body. I just stood there thinking to myself that this man is really here with me and he doesn't care if I don't weigh a hundred. He actually likes me for the sweet giving person that I am and that's what makes me sexy. While I stood there watching him I wondered what is it that he's hiding from me and why don't he talk about himself or family. As I stood in the doorway watching him I heard him clear his throat which means he's waiting for me. I stepped in and he began washing my body and filling me up at the same time. I decided I would take charge of this situation. I turned to face him and dropped to my knees so that his penis was at mouth level. I began sucking his penis and twirling his balls around in my mouth, listening to him moan and enjoying his pleasure. I decided to get rough with him and suck him hard and put my teeth all over his dick. The bathroom was all hot and steamy and so was I. I turned to grab hold to the door and bent over so he could fuck me. I screamed in exasperation as I was cuming and he did to.

CHAPTER 3

Having sex with him was incredible. He knew all the right spots on my body; he knew what to say and how to say it. When morning arrived I found myself alone again. I wonder where he goes while I sleep. I've asked him before he says the same thing to work and he'll see me later. Like a fool I always said okay. The phone ranged. "Hi Denese, how are you? Fine Alex how are you? Fine where are you? At work, okay I miss you. When am I going to see you again? You will see me in a few days. I called to let you know I'm going out of town for business you won't be able to contact me. I will be in meetings all day but I will call you as soon as I get a chance. Ok have a safe trip". Be safe and I'll see you when you return. For the next few days I worked so hard so that I wouldn't think about him but it was really hard. I thought about him all the time and every time I did I could feel myself being turned on. By Friday he was back and I was determine not to work for the weekend. I knew Alex was coming to see me. I got home about 6:00 in the evening and showered. I put on something really sexy that I had just bought. The lighting was set the music was playing. I chilled a bottle of wine and I made sure I had strawberries and cantaloupes and most of all a bottle of chocolate syrup. The doorbell ranged I answered it quickly. I opened the door and there stood one of the sexiest men alive, my Alex. Hi come on in. Alex came in and grabbed me he kissed me gently. I devoured his tongue. I wanted to eat him up. Hi Alex, I take it you missed me about as much as I missed you. Yes I did, would you like a glass of wine? Yes please I've had a long few days and I need to relax. What would you like to do Alex? Lie down and get some sleep? Only if you lay down with me. You're looking sexy tonight are you expecting company? My company is already here, I was waiting for you and only you my sweetie. Come let me run you a hot bath and get you out of those traveling clothes. I missed you so much I just wanted to hold you come on lets go to bed. Alex got undressed and climbed into bed. Being the freak that I am, I brought in the fruit and chocolate syrup, and he could never resist a good fuck. I began to pour syrup on his chest and he was liking every minute of it. Denese I want to talk to you baby. I wouldn't stop licking the syrup off his body, go ahead baby talk. I can't with you licking on me you have chocolate syrup all on my dick. I will suck that off you. I went to the bottom of the bed to lick the chocolate off my man. I sucked all the chocolate off him until he came in my mouth. Denese you don't play fair but now it's my turn. Give me the chocolate. He poured it on my breast he took the strawberries and placed them my nipples. He poured chocolate all the way down to my stomach and stopped. He began licking my breast and he was nibbling on the strawberries. When he started licking the chocolate off my body I was turned on so much. Alex I want to feel you inside of me now? See I told you I just wanted to talk than you had to get me all excited now it's my turn and I'm not ready to fuck yet. I like what I'm doing right now and that's watching you turn red with anticipation. Oh so you want to play dirty. Alex you know I can play dirty as well. No Denese I don't want to play dirty with you. I know you like to tease too much so I'm just going to get right to business. That's what I'm talking about fuck me. We pushed the food and syrup on the floor and he got on top of me and fucked me good. After we finished we just laid there I was wrapped in his arms. Denese I still need to talk to you. I know it's late but I have something I need to tell you. He was serious; I had never seen him like this so I listened to him. My name is Alex Nesbit, I know you know that much. I am fifty years old and I have a wife. A wife so that's where you go at night home to your wife. I sat up in the bed amazed but not shocked. I kind of figured he was married but didn't want to believe it. I was having such a real good time with him. He made me feel more beautiful and sexy than I have felt in a long time. My marriage is not a happy one and I thought that you would be a one night stand but you turned out not to be. When I'm with you I feel so alive and happy. My wife thinks I'm at work whenever I'm with you so I figured before things got to deep you needed to know. I don't want to be like your husband and mistreat you. I find you to be an extraordinary woman. I'm sorry if I hurt you and understand if you never want to see me again, but if you just be a little more patient with me I will be getting a divorce. I've watched you for several weeks sitting in the park crying every day and I was feeling sorry for you. I saw how lonely you looked every day so I decided to introduce myself to you and thought maybe I could make you a one night stand. I thought that all you needed was some sex and you will be fine but I found myself intrigued with you. You weren't like most women I had met and I wanted to keep seeing you. I thought that maybe we could make something out of this and see where it goes. I don't want to lose you Alex; I find myself crazy about you and would like to know more about you. I'm crazy about you to Denese and don't want to lose you either. I know I can make you happy and give you what you need. Come lay down next to me I want to make love to you right now, I want to eat you up. I want that to. He started kissing me gently on my lips he moved around to my ears and started to whisper and I knew it was over. He had me under his spell. His voice is just so dam intoxicating. His breath so sweet and he tasted so good he pulled down my strap off my shoulder and began kissing my sticky skin with his soft lips. His fingers gripped my breast and started to squeeze my big nipples between his two fingers. I moaned and groaned then he removed my other strap and moved on to that breast. I let out a moan with tears in my eyes knowing what I was doing was wrong because this man is married but I didn't want him to stop. He couldn't see my tears it was really dark. He gently moved his hand down my stomach to my vagina and he stroked my clitoris I moaned even heavier I was panting like a puppy in heat. He slid his fingers into my pussy while sucking on my nipples and he began moving his fingers in and out of me I couldn't stand it. Alex fuck me now. Hold on baby I want to play with you some more. His voice was so deep and heavy which turned me on even more. I love the sound of his voice. Alex I'm going to cum I want you to put your dick in me please, oh baby cum on my fingers let me see what you taste like. He kept thrusting his fingers in me he sucked my nipples harder I began to scream, cum baby cum for daddy.

He got harder I got wetter oh Alex I'm Cumming omg here it comes, "ahhhhhhh" all over him like a fountain, good baby that's what papi like to do, make you feel good, well papi you did now let mami make you feel good. I started kissing his face and moved to his sexy soft lips and I listen to him moan and I felt his erection getting hard as steel. I climbed that mountain and begin to ride him. He griped my ass as I rode him. He became rough and tossed me on my back and parted my legs so that he could eat my pussy. I felt his tongue going inside of me. He moved up and I felt his penis thrust inside of me and he pounded me and pounded me all I could do was cum over and over for him. When we were finished I laid there in his arms knowing that he would leave me all alone to go home to his wife. I awoke the next morning and true enough he was gone.

CHAPTER 4

Why am I sleeping with this married man? I just went through something like this with my estrange husband, you see I thought I was the only person in my husband life. When I first met him I was 18 years old and the only experience I had was from someone molesting me. So to sleep with him was not going to happen no time soon. It actually took me about a year to have sex with him and it was special for my first time. I actually understood what sex was, he took his time with me and made love to me. He was really soft and gentle with me. He didn't force me to do anything that I was not ready to do. He had gotten us a beautiful suite at the hotel for my birthday in Atlanta. I walked in the room and there was my favorite German chocolate cake on the table and balloons that said happy birthday and happy Valentine's Day. I get two gifts I was born on a special day. There was food on the table, candles were lit everywhere. He turned off the lights then put my two favorite artists in the DVD player, at that time it was Freddie Jackson and Luther Vandross we sat down and ate and listen to the music. He had taking me to see Freddie Jackson the week prior and Luther Vandross that night. He told me that tonight would be special and it was from beginning to end. We slow danced for a while than he disappeared into the bathroom. He had filled the hot tub with water and Japanese cherry blossom bubble bath and rose petals. I took a nice long hot bath and I wrapped myself in the big bath towel that was on the vanity for me. I walked back into the room and he sat me on the bed and unwrapped my towel. He began to lotion my body. He started with my feet and every time he would lotion my toes he would kiss them, he had very strong hands, he moved up my legs to my thighs. I can feel my pussy getting wetter and throbbing for him. He lotion my arms and shoulders than laid me down on my stomach and lotion and massage my back. It was feeling so good I wanted him to take me. I moan with anticipation of wanting him and he knew it too but he didn't rush it. He wanted me to savor the moment and I did, he turned me over on my back. I slid up to my pillows waiting for him to lay with me but he didn't he knelt down on the floor by the side of the bed and pulled out this box, he said "I love you, I loved you too", he opened the box and there it was a beautiful wedding ring, not engagement ring a wedding ring. I want to marry you and be your husband for the rest of my life. I started to cry and wrapped my arms around him and began kissing him. He put the ring on my finger and started kissing my hand than he moved up my arm and into my face and his kisses were so soft and sensual. I just melted. I am a girl who never had anything growing up. All I ever did was take care of my family. Now I have someone to take care of me and I wouldn't even sleep with him for a whole year. He began sucking on my nipples which were already hard as bricks and he knew that was my spot my legs began to open waiting for him to slid his dick in me. But he kept on licking and sucking every inch of my body I groaned louder and louder with each touch of his tongue and hands. He proceeded to move his tongue to my pussy and he ate me up I came so many times in his face but he never stopped his tongue would go in and out of my pussy, his teeth grabbed my clitoris and he sucked and sucked all I could do was let myself go and take it. Man this feels so good it's like being in another world all by ourselves. We got married about a year later and I swear to you sex got better and better. We had two beautiful kids who were growing fast and getting bigger every day they were two years apart in age, but they wouldn't do anything without the other. We were one big happy family so I thought. I noticed things had started to change after about fifteen years or so of being married. I noticed a change in him, I thought for a while it was me because I had started to work more but I never neglected my duties in the home, I still cooked and cleaned every day and made sure my kids was always taking care of. I made sure he always had breakfast, lunch, and dinner. I made sure he always had clean clothes for work and I tried to keep things spicy in our bedroom.

CHAPTER 5

I noticed how distant he became, he was sneaking around on the phone, being out all day and night, and so, one day out of nowhere he asked me to go to the strip club. I was puzzled but I said sure it might be nice and something for us to do together. Since it had been a long time since we did anything together. We use to have standing date night, but even that had stopped. We would go to dinner and a movie; we would take trips all the time so I had missed that. I've been to a strip club with the girls before but not with my husband so why not go and have a good time. One Friday night we went. He already knew where to go. I didn't question him but I had a lot of thoughts going on in my head. We went in and sat down, I noticed quite a few females were speaking to him and one even brought me over a drink so I asked him how long he had been coming here, of course he said it was his first time, but I knew better than that. I knew that was a lie. There were a lot of women coming over to see if I wanted a lap dance. I said no thank you, I could see the frown on his face once again, I thought what's going on here did he want me to get a lap dance for him or me, did he want to watch these women fondle me and make him all excited? While watching the show there was about three women stripping on stage together and I watched them get naked and fondle each other. They kissed and sucked each other nipples, they ate each other pussy. I could see my husband erection coming through his pants, he was so hard so

I said baby lets go fuck I'm horny and you're hard let's do something about it. We can do it anywhere, so we went to the car I lifted my dress and climbed on him. I didn't wear any panties so it made it real easy to ride him. I fucked him hard it felt so good but I can tell his mind wasn't on me. I turned to him, Charles you are a thousand miles away what's going on what are you thinking about? He said nothing, so we went back into the club for another drink and watched some more of the girls. Charles expression still hasn't changed since I wouldn't agree to a lap dance. As we drove up in our driveway before we got out the car he turned to me and said, I want a threesome, I want you to make love to another woman while I watch and then I want you both to fuck me. I looked at him, "are you serious, you want to fuck someone else and you want me to make love to a woman? Yes I do it will make me happy if you do that for me. Charles that's not me I don't share my man with anyone else and you shouldn't want to share me with anybody. I guess you're not going to do the one thing I ask to make me happy? No Charles I don't see that happening. Would you allow me to fuck another man while you watch? It's not the same thing. Yes it is, you want to fuck other women, but I can't fuck other men we are married, our sex lives are only for us to enjoy. I can see how mad he was getting than he tells me I'm going to the store. I'll be right back; I got out of the car and went into the house he pulled off so fast. Is he really that mad about me not wanting to do a threesome? It's something else to this, but I pushed the idea in the back of my mind. I decided to put on something sexy and put on some sexy music and light some candles so when he get back I can make mad passionate love to him and let him know he only needs me no other woman. I am more than enough for him at least I thought I was, but as time went by he didn't come back, after a few hours I went to bed. It was dam near morning when he decided to come home. I woke up to him putting clothes in the washer and I asked him what he doing? He said washing some clothes; I thought I would help you out. I said ok, but I knew that was kind of funny considering he doesn't wash clothes. So where have you been? I thought you were going to the store and back. I went to the car lots to look at cars you know just riding around; he slipped into the bathroom and locked the door. I went to look in the washing machine to see what was in there, all I saw was his clothes that he had on and a towel. My first thought is he was out fucking somebody else since I wouldn't have the threesome he wanted and now trying to clean up his evidence. So next few days was strange he wouldn't even touch me. When I would come home from work, he would get up and get dressed and leave. He would stay gone until it was time for him to get ready for work. Than he would come home, get changed and leave. He did that for a while so I started leaving too. I would go out to have a few drinks or play at the casino, anything to be out just as long as him. The next few years were the same, but he started having people in my house when I was gone for long periods of time. When he would leave I would start snooping around looking for stuff out of the ordinary. I was finding t-shirts with sperm on them hid in the basement. I started finding sex toys hid in shoe boxes. I would come home to floors vacuumed and bed made, shit he has never done before in life so now my mind is really turning.

CHAPTER 6

So one day I came home from work early, I tried to call him but he never answered. I came in my back door, and behold this man was fucking my very best friend, one who I treated like my sister in my bed, I stood there in shock, all I could do was cry I never said a word to neither one of them, I grabbed my gun, they started running around trying to put on clothes and talking about they could explain. I don't want to hear shit yall got to say. I let my best friend move in because she was having problems at home so I figured I could help her out. But who knew these two bitches would start fucking in my house right under my nose. By the time they got outside I unloaded every bullet I had at them. I didn't want to go to jail so trust me I missed on purpose. I turned around and went back into the house and started grabbing up my sheets off the bed, clothes and towels. I went outside and started a fire, I burned everything I could get to burn. I had so much going through my mind, I didn't know what to do or what to think so I decided to take a late night walk. I found that I had walked ten miles and came to this freeway over pass. I put one leg across the cement barrier and sat on the concrete pillar and just cried. I kept asking why or how he could do this to me, not having a threesome led to this bull shit, or he just wanted to fuck someone else in general. No it wasn't the threesome this man has been fucking around on me all along. What have I done wrong? I kept the house cleaned; I cooked everyday even made breakfast before work. I made sure he always had clean work clothes. I took care of the kids did all the school stuff. I worked and paid bills, any kind of vehicle he wanted I went and got in my name for him, from cars, trucks, motorcycles anything he wanted. I bought his clothes, jewelry everything. He never had to go to the store for anything. I went to the strip club with him, whatever this man wanted I did for him so why did he fuck me over like this than. My phone ranged and shook me out of my thoughts; it was an older female friend of mine that I thought of as my sister. I didn't answer so she kept calling so I finally answered and these words came out of her mouth, Denese whatever you're going through God can fix it for you. I never even said hello or anything. It was like she knew something was wrong with me, she kept talking and I found myself walking back home clearing my head. I end up staying a few more months. One night I decided to move out. I started looking at apartments until I found one I was comfortable with. I packed up all my shit and left. I found myself depressed and stressed out my weight was going up and down, I went to work depressed and quiet but I did my job 100% just never had a conversation with anybody that was not work related. I started taking walks every day and found myself at this park; it was so beautiful and peaceful. I would go there to think about my life and what have I done to inflict so much pain upon myself. What have I done wrong? Why couldn't this man love me? Was I getting too fat for him? Was it that I'm not sexy to him? What was it? What was wrong with me? After about a few months of me leaving my husband is when I met Alex. At first he would speak to me and keep walking but most of the time I was in tears so I would just wave as he walked by until the day he decided to sit on the bench I was sitting on and ask me that question, would you like some company? My first thought was he was a dog and just wanted to get in my panties, and on one hand I didn't even care. Why not become a hoe seems like most of the women and men I knew were hoes anyway but when he opened his mouth and I heard that deep sensual voice I fell under his spell. But then as time went on I wondered if maybe he found me attractive and was he going to be a good man for me. In the back of my mind I wondered why someone who is sexy as hell wants someone like me. Why did this man approach me? He was breath taking and smelled so good; when he came to me I was intrigued. When we talked on that first day it was like he was really interested in me. I fell for him hook line and sinker. After talking to Alex for a few months I found out he was married, like I said all men are dogs but by then I was so into him and how he made me feel when he was with me. I didn't care I couldn't have my man alone so why should any other woman have their man alone. That's the part of my life I wished I could have taking back being so cold about other women and their man. My husband had this hold on me. So I picked up this bitter attitude after the way he treated me and for what he did to me I hated all men so my philosophy was like this, "I don't care" someone had fucked over me so I was gone do it to someone else and in my heart I knew it was wrong but I did it anyway.

CHAPTER 7

My birthday was approaching and I didn't have plans. I was used to my husband having plans for me. I really got to get this man out of my mind, so anyway Alex asked me what I wanted to do. I said it doesn't matter he said he wanted to take me out of town for the weekend of course I said yes, but then I thought what about your wife Alex? How can you be gone for a weekend? He said I got that handled I'll just tell her I have a business trip. I really want to take you some where special so you can enjoy your special day. I was excited but knew it wasn't right but wanted someone to take me somewhere to get my mind off the problems that were going on in my life. I really didn't care who it was, it just turned out to be this married man. He would always say his marriage was having all these problems and it was always his wife fault so I believed everything this man said like a fool. As the weeks went by leading up to my birthday I still didn't know where we was going or what to pack so when Alex came over Friday I asked him, where are we going for my birthday so I will know how to pack, just pack for fun in the sun ok, but where I mean do I need many clothes do I need a bathing suit? Knowing a two piece was out of the question until my body get into shape. Tell me more information about where we are going. He said clothing is optional most days but you need something elegant for the night of your birthday. I have some special plans for you. If you like, bring any kind of bathing suit you want. I think you're sexy in anything you put on even if you don' think so. The weather is going to be beautiful day and night. I had two weeks left for my birthday so I wanted something new for this trip and went shopping. I bought new bra and panties for this occasion and some new outfits. I was so excited I made sure my vacation days were in for that Friday and Monday. I knew I would need an extra day to recuperate. Finally my birthday weekend was here. Alex picked me up Friday morning for our trip. As we drove on the freeway toward the airport. I sat there wandering about the lie he told his wife and how many lies did my husband tell me every time he walked out the door. I wondered how many women had he taken out of town or just spent the night with while I sat at home taking care of the kids and the house. When we arrived at the airport I asked Alex do you think this is right lying to your wife to be with your girlfriend. Denese don't worry about it me and her have been seeing other people for a while we haven't been happy with each other in a long time. But Alex I still feel strange about this I don't want to hurt your wife I know how it feels to think you're in love with someone and find out later it's only a one way street. Dense you are what's important to me right now I love you and want you to be happy so can you please go with me and enjoy the weekend. I was in a state of shock he just said he love me. I didn't see that coming so with a big smile on my face proceeded through the airport hand in hand. When we reached the counter I heard the attendant say now boarding first class to Miami. I said Miami that's where we going. Yes beautiful that's where we going south beach. While in first class Alex had ordered champagne for the both of us we tapped glasses and he said happy birthday baby this is going to be a wonderful weekend just wait and see. When we landed there was a limousine waiting for us to take us to our hotel room with more champagne in the car. When we reached the hotel the bellman took our bags while we checked in. We got on the elevator and I reached over and gave Alex the most sensual kiss I could. When the elevator reached the top floor I was in awe the penthouse suite overlooking the beach. The views were awesome all around I felt like a child in the candy store. As I looked around the room I noticed beautiful roses all over the place in all colors. There was roses all over the bed Alex grabbed me around my waist and pulled me into him and he started kisses me down the side of my face around to my lips than his tongue slide down my neck. I could feel the shivers all over my body my nipples were hard as bricks my pussy was all hot and wet. He whispered in my ear lets shower and get ready for dinner and walked off. I was standing there waiting for him to throw me on the bed and fuck my brains out but that didn't happen so I took off my stilettos and walked into the bathroom. Alex was waiting for me so I decided since he left me hanging I will give him a strip tease show and make him all hot and bothered. There was real nice soft sexy music playing over the intercom system. He turned on the shower and started taking off his clothes. I started undoing my buttons on my shirt slowly while swaying my hips to the beat of the music he looked up and sat down on the edge of the tub. I could see he was getting exciting as I unzipped my skirt and let it fall softly on the floor. He was smiling so big showing his pearly white teeth and sexy dimples on the side of his cheeks. I could see the budge in his pants I turned away from him with my back facing him. I gently slide my bra straps down my shoulder one strap at a time. Then I unfasten it and let it fall to the floor while still swaying to the music and not turning around to see his face. I bent over so that all he could see was my ass I gently glide my panties down my legs to take them off. By the time I got ready to turn around Alex was on me. You are so sexy I don't know why that man cheated on you. I don't want to talk about him this weekend at all Alex this is my special time and I want it to be just for me with no regrets ok baby. He began caressing my body rubbing up against me licking me down my back, this feels so good Alex don't stop he grabbed my hand and led me over by the tub where he sat down and pulled me over him as to where my pussy was in his face. He put one of my legs on his shoulder and he started kissing my inner thigh as his tongue was gliding up and down my thigh to my leg I felt like I was about to faint. He then reached my clit and he began sucking and licking me. I could feel myself weakening for him he pulled me down on him and began licking my breast. I unzipped his pants and slid down on his dick he was so hard and I was oh so wet. I rode him hard all while listening to him pant and moan giving it to him like he never had it before my bounces got harder and I stroked him tightening my pussy muscles around his dick making him weak in the knees. I could feel him cuming and knew it was time and we panted and panted until we reached our climax together. It was so explosive and hot and so was the bathroom. We finally got into the shower. When Alex finished he returned back to the bedroom, I followed right behind him. Alex started getting ready for dinner and I noticed he had laid out his Armani suit black of course. He looks so good in black but hell I love anything he put on even if he's just naked. I thought to myself I don't have anything that glamorous to put on but then I heard a knock on the door. I'll get it baby. I headed back to the bathroom to lotion up and put on my makeup. Alex never said a word he kept getting dressed I came out to the sexiest dress I had ever had in my life laying on the bed. I had tears in my eyes. Is this really for me Alex? Yes a beautiful dress for my beautiful queen now put it on we have reservations and the car will be here soon. All I could do was grab him and kiss him. Thank you so much I love it I took off my robe and grab my sexy bra and panties and put them on. I stepped into my dress I felt like I was really special feelings I haven't had in a long time was stirred up in me. We headed out the door to our elevator. The front entrance of the hotel was so elegant and beautiful I thought I was in a fairytale. It had a lot of shops and restaurants. I thought we were having dinner there but Alex made reservations at the colonnade room for us, which was a really expensive restaurant where all the rich and famous go and the celebrities were out as well. When I walked in I saw so many famous people and people were speaking to Alex as if he was as famous also. He introduced me as his friend that's out celebrating her birthday and I agreed with him and just smiled. I didn't want to ruin my evening by saying I'm his girlfriend. The maîtred escorted us to a private table overlooking others. There was no one within ear shot of us. The waiter came out with some wine that Alex had already preordered than our salads came out. I have always been a funny eater but Alex knew what I liked. My salad was just the way I like it lettuce, tomatoes and Italian dressing. It was perfect and it was so good. I've never been a steak eater but Alex had ordered me a rib eye with cheese fries. I was amazed that he paid that much attention to me to remember what I like to eat. After we ate dinner we were serenaded with the most beautiful music coming out of the mouth of none other than Freddie Jackson. One of my favorite singers of all time the music was so beautiful and sensual I could feel my inner thighs getting all wet and the tingle in my secret area. I knew he sensed it I can tell by the smile on his face. Why are you smiling so much Alex? I like the look on your face Denese you seem to be so happy and enjoying yourself and it makes me happy to. He moved in closer to me and planted a nice kiss on my lips. I was like a little child who just won the big prize from a carnival. After Freddie Jackson finish serenading us the waiter brought out some more wine. The restaurant continues to play Freddie's music over the speaker. Alex then began to run his fingers up my thighs I was so turned on already one touch I was going to cum all over his fingers anyway. He kept going all I could hear than was the sound of my own heart beating. I slowly opened my legs for him he played with my clit moving his fingers all around me then I could feel his fingers slide into me, oh Alex lets go back to the hotel room, oh no baby I want you to cum right here at this table for me. I want to feel your squirt on my fingers so I can taste your sweet sexy fluids. He kept moving in and out of my pussy. My moans became louder and my panting became stronger. I tried to hold myself but I couldn't the force of his hand and fingers were so magical that he knew exactly what to do. Oh Alex you're going to make me cum right here and now, he whispered cum baby cum for me he put his mouth on mine and he kept going. I let out a loud scream and came all over his hand. He began kissing me hard trying to stop my screaming I could feel the warmness coming out of my body the pleasure was too much to handle but I let it all go all over his hand. Alex why would you do that to me here? I feel all wet now, don't worry about it baby I want you to have a weekend to remember and I'm going to make sure every chance I get you have a good time and a good orgasm. Thank you so much for everything Alex. We headed back to the limousine hand in hand.

CHAPTER 8

We rode back to our hotel room when we reached our floor he gave me a big kiss and led me off the elevator into our room. When he opened the door I saw this cake sitting on the table it happen to be my favorite German chocolate cake and some more beautiful roses, oh thank you Alex you thought of everything. I leaned in to give him a kiss after we turned each other a loose I told him I needed to take a shower and went into the bathroom to turn on the water. I took a nice hot shower when I turned the water off I heard Alex cell phone rang. I stayed in the bathroom not to bother him but I was listening to his words. I was wondering who would be calling at this late hour so I stood in the door to hear. I could hear him saying yes baby my flight went fine I've been in meetings all day that's why I haven't called and right now I'm tired got an early meeting in the morning so I'll call you tomorrow I love you too. I knew what I was getting myself into when I got involved with a married man. I believed him when he said their marriage was over and that he didn't love her but I guess I was only fooling myself sounds like the same lies my husband would tell me when I called him when he said he had to go out of town for a meeting. So I stood in the mirror with tears in my eyes wondering what the hell I am doing here. What do this man want from me? Am I some project he felt sorry for? What were his plans? I wiped my face and returned to the bedroom wrapped in my towel. I went to the closet to fine my nightie cause now I wanted to go to bed he saw the look on my face, honey what's wrong look like you've been crying, nothing I just washed my face I'm kind of tired and want to lie down ok baby I'm going to take a shower be out soon. I laid in the bed trying to be sleep before he came out but I started to cry all over again and by the time his shower was over I was still awake I had turned off all the lights so it was dark when he came to bed. I could see his shadow from the moonlight as he slipped on his pajama pants he eased into the bed. I turned my back to him he leaned over and said Denese what's wrong your demeanor has changed since your shower talk to me and tell me what's wrong. I turned to face him and said I heard your phone conversation and gathered that was your wife, yes it was her why what did you hear? I heard you tell her you were in meetings all day and that you loved her. Yes I did tell her that and I'm sorry that you heard it but you have to understand from my point of view we don't have a marriage I don't love her anymore. So why did you say that to her? Why do you have to lie about where you are and what you're doing if your marriage is over? Dense I haven't had a chance to really sit down and tell her I want a divorce yet just give it time and when we get back I will tell her and the only reason I said I love you was so she can get off the phone. Once again I believed him. He put his arms around me to hold me. But for some one reason I still was crying I guess I knew in the back of my mind he was lying so I cried myself to sleep. The next morning I realize I was alone in bed so I got up and went to the bathroom to freshen up. When I came out, I walked into the kitchen and there sat Alex at the table he had ordered breakfast and was waiting for me he greeted me with a good morning kiss. I sat down next to him and once again he had my favorite waffles and sausages with orange juice and he had the same thing except he had eggs over easy, baby are you alright this morning yes Alex I'm fine ok well when you get done we are going down to the beach for a while. Alex I really don't feel like the beach today can we go later I just want to stay in for a while. No we are going to the beach to hang out and get a couple of drinks and enjoy one another so finish your breakfast and get ready to go. I looked at him like he had lost his mind. Alex, don't Alex me get up and get ready to go. So I went to the room to put on my bathing suit and my wrap and headed for the door he was standing there waiting for me he took me by my hand and pulled me into him. I love you and I want you to be happy especially this weekend doesn't let that phone call ruin our trip lets go swimming the water is beautiful you will love it, ok Alex lets go. We headed to the elevator and got on we went down to the pool side first and sat at the bar where he ordered me a peach margarita and him a cold beer we sat there and had our drinks we found two chairs by the poolside under an umbrella. Pass me some sun screen please baby I opened my purse and to my dismay there was a box gift wrapped in my purse. Alex when did you put this in my purse? I did it in the elevator when I pulled you close to me. I opened the box and it was a gorgeous diamond tennis bracelet, omg this is beautiful it's too expensive you didn't have to buy me a gift you brought me on this beautiful trip that was more than enough for me, baby its yours I want you to have it here let me put it on your wrist. Thank you so much I love it, now pass me the sun screen so I can rub down your body don't need that pretty brown skin getting burned so. I laid face down on my lawn chair and he started to rub my back his hands are so strong and yet so soft even his rubbed downs was enjoyable all the way down to my toes once he finished the back side I turned over to let him do the front of my body now he wanted to get freaky with me he want to start pulling on my nipples instead of rubbing my arms. Ok Alex don't start anything down here at this pool. I grabbed him by the hand lets go swimming we went into the water, there was quite a few people there but not that crowded. I eased him into a corner of the pool and started to kiss him on his neck down to his chest. I turned to put my butt on him I could feel him rising so I turned back around. Alex seem like you have something else in mind or should I say your dick has something else in mind. Alex slid my bikini bottom to the side to where he could slide himself into me and I guess since everybody was coupled up and nobody was really paying us any attention we continued on with our sexcapade in the water and it felt good I made him cum all in me. Alex was a man that I couldn't resist his charm and his voice just melted me every time he spoke. We continued to have fun in the water it started getting late I knew I had to pack for our trip back to reality in the morning so I suggested to Alex that we head to our room of course he said let's stay a little longer they have a firework show. I want us to sit down by the beach so let's head down there to get a good spot. As we approached the beach there was a lot of people there on the sand laughing and talking and of course drinking bad having a good time. We found a nice spot not too far from the water and took a seat I noticed some nice looking guys on the beach and some all alone just enjoying the water. Alex went to get us some drinks and I noticed out the corner of my eye a guy was taking pictures and he took one of me. I looked at him and smiled he was sexy but then Alex appeared and said oh you like that, of course I do a sexy man taking my picture along with everyone else I felt flattered. Alex sat down and gave me my drink I could see that he was still bothered but why he has a wife at home and I'm all alone at home. I thought it was funny he got a little jealous. The fireworks has started and they were gorgeous and loud but the show was spectacular but I could feel someone watching me and I looked around to find that hunk of a man who took my picture looking at me and he smiled I didn't know rather to smile or be scared could he be a stalker or a crazy person. I turned my attention back to Alex he seemed to be enjoying himself, Alex grabbed me by the hand and pulled me up from the sand, let's go baby time to go back to our room okay as we walked hand in hand that guy was still looking at us. I got closer to Alex we walked passed him when we reached the elevator I asked Alex did he know that guy that took my picture and kept looking at us, he said no he never saw him a day before in his life. So I wiped it out of my mind. I went to the bathroom to turn on the water in the tub and put in my favorite bubble bath, Japanese cherry blossom. Once the tub finish filling up I took off my swim suit and got in. I slid down to relax and closed my eyes I was interrupted by Alex who had a glass of wine in his hand and slid down behind me. I laid against his chest. Denese I hope you had a good and relaxing weekend but most of all I hope you enjoyed your birthday. Yes Alex I did and thank you so much for it all. Well if you really want to thank me turn around and face me so I did I straddled myself across his lap and leaned in to give him a sensual kiss. I could feel him rising up against me so I took my sponge to give him a bath but he stopped me in mid drift and leaned in to suck my breast. I could feel the heat between us and we started to have sex in the tub when we were done and finally took our bath he got out the tub to his phone ringing. I stepped out to listen to his conversation and realize once again it was his wife he was talking in riddles but once again I did hear him say I love you too every time I hear him say that to her it's like a knife sticking in my chest. I got dressed for bed because we had an early flight back to Chicago.

CHAPTER 9

The morning came, it was time to get up and get ready to go. I awoke to breakfast in bed, it smelled so good and a cup of coffee was just what I needed. After breakfast we headed to the limo to take us back to the airport and I have to say for the ride home I was looking good. Once we arrived at the airport and got checked in we had some time before our flight was to leave. I noticed this guy was looking at me and it was the same sexy hunk of a man I saw at the pool and the beach. I felt a little shaken but he flashed his gorgeous smile all I could see was his sexy white teeth and his sexy dimple. He pnly had one dimple in his face. We boarded the plane in first class this guy was on the same plane but he was in coach. I wondered what was going on with this man, we landed at O'Hare airport and went to retrieve our luggage and headed to the parking deck to get the car. We arrived back at my apartment Alex said he had to run some errands he will see me later I knew what that meant he had to go smooth things out with his wife, but it was cool I had some calls to make myself. After checking my answering machine and realize how full it was I never told anyone but my mother and my big sister that I was going out of town for my birthday. I called my mom to make sure she was alright and told her about my trip how much fun it was she was glad to hear it but before she hung up she said be careful of that man I have a strange feeling about him. Don't let him hurt you like your husband has done, watch your feelings for this man this could back fire in your face. I knew she was right, I love you mom and I will but now I need to call my big sister bye for now. I called my big sister Diane, hey Denese did you check your lotto numbers I know the numbers you play and if you played them before you left you are a millionaire. I've been calling you because I know you hit. I haven't check them I just got back into town, well go check and call me back. So I checked and true enough I had hit the largest jackpot ever and all by myself. I called my sister back, Diane you were right and I hit it all by myself so don't tell anyone I don't want people calling me. I already know what I'm going to do with it and you know I will take care of you after I take care of my kids and mom and dad. I know you will but don't worry about me you buy the things in life you want and take care of your kids and their families I just want to see you happy. That's how I became a millionaire. I will call you back to tell you about my birthday weekend, ok handle your business first talk to you soon and sis congratulations you deserve it all thanks Diane I love you, love you too bye. When she hung up I just sat there in total shock. I hurried up and locked up my ticket in my safe so I could go turn it in the morning. I went to the kitchen to pour me a glass of wine I was so excited I couldn't believe what has happen to me. I am now one of the wealthiest people in the world. The first thing I'm going to do is get me a penthouse apartment in downtown Chicago. I had so many ideas as to what I was going to do with the money. I wonder if I should tell Alex of my good news or should I just keep it quiet like Diane told me. I called Diane back after my heart stop racing, Hello Diane how are you? I'm fine and yourself, I'm wonderful as well, so how did your trip go? It was really good except when his wife called and I had to listen to him lie about where he was and whom he was with. I told you be careful something's not right I know but he told me he was falling in love with me and that he was going to divorce his wife so we could be together, so what did you do? I had the most beautiful time I've had in a long time he had everything planned out to the tee he didn't leave any stone unturned it was great. He gave me a great diamond and tennis bracelet he wine and dine me the whole weekend and when he made love to me I felt like I was in another world. Okay I don't want to hear about that keep all that to yourself but listen to me you know how you went through all this deception with your husband well it's the same thing he doing to his wife you didn't like it being done to you so don't do it to her. I know you just want to be happy but do it with a man who is single I hear you Diane and I promise to be careful.

CHAPTER 10

The next morning I called in to my job and told them I couldn't make it in. I went to the lottery office about my pay day I told them I don't want to be on TV and I don't want my name in the papers none of that I want to stay low key and they did just that. After I received my first check I went straight downtown to this high rise apartment building and took the penthouse suite. Than I went to the furniture store and bought all new furniture and everything. I decided to move by the weekend, than I went to the state building to find out how to buy the court building I was working in and I bought it so I could revamp it and get rid of people who weren't doing a good job when I was working with them. I decided to change the head of the staff I knew about all their underhanded deals and no longer required their services I was on a roll. I called my kids and told them they had a substantial amount of money deposited into their bank accounts from me and to buy whatever they wanted to they didn't even have to work anymore if they didn't want to it was up to them but since they were both in the service and loved it I knew they were going to stay but they didn't have to worry about finances. That evening Alex came over and I told him I was moving, why baby why are you moving is something wrong with your apartment, no I'm just moving, ok where are you moving to? I got a penthouse downtown, a penthouse wow you're moving on up how did that happen? Let's just say I came into a large fortune, well good for you need any help, and no I'm good not taking anything with me but my clothes. Well congratulations to you babe lets go out and celebrate, why don't we just stay in and celebrate, we can do that to what you want to do? You know what I want to do? Mmmmmm sounds like a plan to me, he began kissing me passionately his tongue traveling down my body while he was taking my clothes off, he reached my breast which my nipples were already hard and he began to suck on them one at a time. I was so turned on my sexy man, he then began to unzip my skirt and take it off it fell to the floor. He noticed my stockings instead of taking them off he ripped them off and put his hands in my panties and began to stroke my pussy. He laid me down on the couch and put my legs over his shoulders he pulled my panties to the side and began to lick my clitoris's and put his fingers in my pussy and began to fuck me with his fingers, oh Alex you're going to make me cum. I want you now he got up and climbed on top of me and put his dick in me. At first it was nice and slow but as I began to get wetter he got harder and harder he thrust in and out of me all while rubbing my clit making me cum even more, Alex I'm cuming Alex here it comes and we let go together, it feels extra good when we can come together. He laid there on top of me for a minute we both were out of breath after a few minutes his muscles was heavy on my body. Alex I need you to get up now you're smashing my breast, ha-ha I'm sorry baby lets go take a shower so we can get something to eat. Ok I turned on the shower water we stepped in he began to wash my body and started to play with my nipples again. Alex I don't know if I can take anymore of you right now, yes you can you just don't know it yet, you're right I don't know it yet when he finished washing my body I started to wash him I don't think there was any flaws in his body. Alex you are so sexy, so are you Denese. No I'm not I use to be but not anymore, Denese look in this mirror, you are a gorgeous woman from head to toe there is nothing about your body to be ashamed of do you hear me. Alex I could use some toning and to lose some weight I know you're just saying that to be nice. No Denese I mean exactly what I said there is nothing wrong with you now if you want to tighten up your body you don't do it for me do it for yourself I'm happy with it I love it. I walked out the bathroom into my bedroom to find me something to put on Alex followed me and stood behind me and began kissing my back and my neck, his hands grabbing my breast and squeezing my nipples. Denese I like what I see in the back as well as the front now bend over and let me show you how much I do, he began to fuck me from behind all I had to hold on to was the wall and I was climbing the wall too he was hitting it so hard but in a good way when he finished all I could do was hold the wall so I wouldn't fall, fucking Alex was just amazing all the time. This time we did get dressed and I headed to the kitchen. Alex sat down to watch TV, Alex would you like a something to eat, yes if you're fixing something other than grilled chicken salad, actually I made a real nice dinner, fried chicken, yams, greens, dressing, and mac and cheese, how's that, that sounds really food hell yea I want some. I'll come in the kitchen so we can sit down at the table and talk, ok that's fine I'll make you a plate. We sat down and had a real nice conversation about my move and what I was going to do with my apartment and my first investment. I actually own the building I couldn't believe that, well baby if you need any help just let me know I can help in any way of running a business like that. I will I think I would be alright I have my master's degree in business, now it's time to put it to good use but if I need any advice I will come to you. That's a deal, our dinner was over and Alex had to go, Denese I have to go but I will see you tomorrow ok Alex see you tomorrow. I decided that since my apartment was actually ready the next day I was going to move I didn't have much clothes so I put them in my car and gathered up my personal item and packed them all up and a few more items. I already told my landlord I was moving and was going to leave everything there so he can rent it out furnished. The furniture I had was not bad at all and I did buy it new the only thing was wrong was I fucked on it a few times but all in all it was still new never had much company so practically everything in there was still kind of new. The morning came I was so excited about moving into my new place. Alex called to say good morning I told him I was moving and gave him my address to where I was going to be, now I'm all moved in and the first thing I needed to do was grocery shopping all my new furniture had arrived and was set up even my dishes were in the cabinets. The concierge took care of everything for me, on my way to the grocery store I came upon the Mercedes dealer. I need a new car and know exactly what I want, Mercedes Benz S-class, in black with black leather interior with tinted windows and that's what I bought. I told the dealer to have it delivered to my address I will be waiting for it, so I left to continue my journey to my new home. Alex came by to check out my new place and while he was there my car was delivered, we went outside so I could sign for it and park it in the garage, dam Denese nice car babe who helped you pick it out, nobody I learned about cars with my husband and since I was never able to get what I wanted now I can. Well baby it looks good now you stomping with the big dogs, you're funny lets go back in, ok let's go. We went back into the building Alex was really impressed with my place but I know he's use to this even bigger than this. Ok baby I have a meeting I just came by to check you out, he leaned in to kiss me his tongue devoured my mouth it was so passionate. After he left there was someone at my door. I thought it was Alex coming back, so I went to the intercom, yes may I help you, yes my name is Jason and I'm a private investigator I need to talk to you may I come in please, just one second before I let him in I went to retrieve my gun never know who at the door so I slid my gun in my thigh holster under my skirt and buzzed him in when he reached my door I looked through the peep hole and realize this is the same man I saw in Miami so before I opened the door I asked him why are you following me? Who and what do you want? Mrs. Taylor my name is Jason Domenico I am a private investigator I need to talk you please let me in I won't hurt you here is my id and badge so I opened the door and invited him in. What can I do for you Mr. domencio I don't understand why you here, Mrs. Taylor I work for Mrs. Nesbit Alex Nesbit wife she hired me a while ago to follow him that's why you saw me in Miami my job is to take pictures and report back to her, so why are you telling me this, because Mrs. Taylor you are an innocent bystander in this game. When I first saw you I found myself attracted to you and wondered how did you get in this with him. I couldn't help but stare at him while he was talking he was a fine Italian stud of a man I didn't really hear much of what he was saying. Mrs. Taylor are you listening to me? Yes I'm sorry go on continue with what you were saying, Mr. domenico, Mrs. Nesbit is very rich and if she suspects that her husband is cheating he won't get a dime of her money in the divorce so she needed proof so she hired me. I came to you without her knowing because this man is only going to hurt you he will never leave his wife for you if he do he will be flat broke he can't afford that he used to this lavish life style. So actually I'm here to help you so you won't be hurt, I don't know what to say he told he they were having problems and that he didn't love her. Mrs. Taylor don't be fooled by this man he loves his wife maybe not all the time but trust me he loves her. Can you tell me how did you come to meet Mr. Nesbit? I met him one day in the park during my most vulnerable stage in my life he seemed so nice and after spending so much time with him I started to fall in love with him and I thought he was in love with me at least he told me he was. Mrs. Taylor I do apologize for all this but you're not the first vulnerable woman he has approached. Thank you for all the information but can you please leave I need some time to think. Than my phone alerted me with a message and it was from Alex saying, hey sweetie did too much playing this weekend have to work late I will call you tomorrow goodnight my love. I looked at the private investigator and he said he's not coming tonight he has to stay home and spend time with his wife. Please can you leave now I opened the door I could feel my eyes swelling up with tears he left?

CHAPTER 11

I slammed the door and went to the couch where I was crying my eyes out. I thought this man was really going to leave his wife for me and all this money he was spending on me was all hers he has nothing. I could deal with the fact that he's broke I have my own money hell I have enough for us both so what he was going to leave her for me and then take my money and spend it on some other woman this shit is so crazy so now what do I do. I went to my bedroom to lay down I guess I was really exhausted cause when I woke up it was morning so I went into the bathroom to shower and get ready for work, when I arrived to my office I noticed a bouquet of roses on my desk, they were absolutely beautiful and the card read" I'm so sorry" if you need anything call me here is my number, from Frank Domenico. I put the card in my desk and began to work I had a lot of meetings schedule so I threw myself into my day. I noticed about 5 o'clock I haven't heard from Alex all day so I decided to call him, but there was no answer it went straight to voice mail. I didn't leave a message so I decided to call my sister Diane to see if she wanted to go out to dinner with me. Hello sis how are you? I wanted to know if you wanted to meet me for dinner and drinks, yes sure I'm almost done with my work so I will meet you at wolf gang puck, ok see you there.

CHAPTER 12

I was walking to the parking garage when I saw Alex on the corner with the passenger door open to his car, Alex what are you doing here? I needed to see you and couldn't wait any longer can we go to your place, no Alex I'm on my way to meet my sister for dinner what's wrong, nothing I've been working all day trying to catch up on some work and just needed to see you, I haven't heard from you since early yesterday, so I guess you had to spend time with your wife, I tell you what when I'm done with my sister I will call you on my way home to see what you want to do. Well at least let me take you to your car, ok I got in the passenger seat and he closed the door behind me and came around to the driver seat and got in. when we reached my car he leaned in to kiss me, of course I couldn't resist. I was all in he was just so sexy. I got into my car and drove off. When I reached the restaurant I pulled into valet and got out, Diane was there already at the table waiting for me. I sat down and ordered me a drink than Diane started with her questions about Alex I couldn't bring myself to tell her about the private investigator so I spent the whole time raving about my trip with Alex, I received a text message and when I opened it I saw it was Frank and said I hope you like the flowers with a smiley face at the end. I was wondering how he got my number but with his job I guess he has excess to any information he wanted. So Denese who is that on the phone Alex, no Diane just a friend about work. I brushed her off that subject real quick. After a couple of drinks and dinner was over it was time for us to head home my sister had to go get her grandbaby so her daughter could go to work, ok sis kiss my nephew and tell him his auntie loves him and I will see him soon, bye sis I love you and don't worry about me I have learned my lesson with men, bye Denese love you too.

CHAPTER 13

After my car arrived, I headed for the freeway to go home than my phone rang and it was frank again so I answered it, hello Mr. domenico what can I do for you, and by the way thank you for the roses they are beautiful, hello Mrs. Taylor I just wanted to check on you to make sure you are alright, yes I'm fine, so tell me what is your angle, why are you so interested in what happens to me? isn't that messing with your job you were hired to do, well Mrs. Taylor I find you very attractive and stunning and would like to get to know you better, is something wrong with that, I don't know how many women have you wanted to get to know in your line of work Mr. domenico, first off please call me frank and secondly you are the second woman I wanted to get to know, so what happen to the first she found something wrong with you and left or did you cheat on her and she found out, no not at all I tell you what why don't you meet me for a night cap and we can talk about it, why don't you just come to my place and I'll fix us some coffee okay I'll see you shortly. I pulled into my apartment valet and got out the car and headed for the elevator low and behold there was frank standing at the elevator, so how did you beat me here to my own house. I actually was here when I was talking to you on the phone so what are you stalking me no Mrs. Taylor I was following Mr. Nesbit he came to your apartment. Why he knew I would be out with my sister I don't think he believed you he's been here ever since he left your job he just left maybe five minutes ago Mrs. Taylor you really need to be careful he can be dangerous if he don't get what he wants. So how can he be a danger to me but scared of his wife. Come on lets head upstairs to my apartment I need to get more comfortable. We got on the elevator and headed to the top floor once the doors open I saw a note on my door I took it off and went into my house. I couldn't wait to get out of my shoes today so I invited Frank to have a seat and went into the kitchen to make coffee, how do you like your coffee Mr. I mean Frank. Like I like my women strong with a hint of sugar and cream I laughed at him okay I got it I returned to the living room with the coffee and sat down on the sofa, so tell me Frank what happen to the woman in your life. It's a long story well we have coffee and cookies and if need it we have wine. Well her name was Theresa and she was the love of my life we've spent twenty years together and one day I noticed a change in her, she was disappearing, her clothes and hair changed she was dressing more sexy like she did when we first met. I thought she was trying to get my attention she was always sexy to me but the last few years we learned she couldn't have kids and it really depressed her. I told her we could adopt or figure out something but it wasn't what she wanted she wanted to give me kids from her womb, well anyway one day I went to surprise her at work and she wasn't there so the next day the same thing went to her job she wasn't there so I decided to follow her one morning she went to work that morning and left for lunch. I followed her to a restaurant where she was meeting someone so when he arrived I saw them kiss. I was stunned this went on for a few months so I started taking pictures of all their encounters. I started monitoring her phone calls and text messages I was so wrapped up in seeing what she was doing. I forgot about my life. One day Theresa came home with a busted lip and I asked her what happen she said she bumped her face in the bathroom another time she came home with bruises on her body and tried to hide them from me a few more time she came home with something wrong and she thought she was hiding but I knew better she would start an argument with me just so she can sleep in the guest room so one night when she called herself sneaking out I was already in my car waiting for her to leave. she arrived at the Hilton hotel there I saw the guy who she had been seeing and he took her by the hand and they got on the elevator being the smooth guy I was I flirted with the girl behind the desk to find out who he was and what room they were in and she told me so. I took the adjoining room next to there's I could hear them having sex I started to cry. I couldn't believe she would do this all because we couldn't have a baby. The next thing I knew I heard some yelling and a hard slap he told her the next time he called she better answer and be available, he kept on hitting her and she kept saying she was sorry and she loved him. I busted into the room and saw her swollen face and bruised body lying on the bed. I pulled my gun on him and called the police and ambulance for my wife, he was arrested and she was taking to the hospital. I went with her they gave her something to help her sleep through the night. I just sat there and watched her sleep. By morning when she woke up she looked in my face with tears in her eyes to say I'm so sorry for all this I wanted to give you a child and when I couldn't I didn't feel sexy to you anymore. Being able to bring a child in this world is the sexiest thing in a woman's life and I couldn't do that for you. Theresa how could you cheat on me and of all people a man who was beating you. I never put my hands on you. I always treated you like my queen, she just cried louder we can talk when we get home Theresa. The doctor came in and said we could go home there was no broken bones just rest for the next few days and she will be fine so I helped her get dressed and we left. When we arrived home I took her to the bedroom. And what she did was amazing, she started packing her suitcase to leave me. Theresa why are you leaving we can work through this I can forgive you we can start new. But she said she couldn't live like this anymore and left. I went to find the man that had done this to my wife so I went to his home and his wife came to the door. I was so angry I asked her where was her husband and of course he was not there, she let me in trying to calm me down as I looked through the house I saw all the pictures on the wall of them together so I asked her, do you know your husband cheats on you and beat the women that he cheats with, I had my suspicions that he was cheating but I didn't know the extent of his violent rage. Well he was sleeping with my wife and he beat her several times and now she has left me and I'm looking for him. Please sir have a seat and let's talk, may I get you a drink or something. I was in tears not knowing what to do or where she was at or where he was at. Ma'am do you mind if I ask you a question, sure do your husband beat you, he used to but after I took self-defense class and a gun class and had to defend myself with him he learned to never put his hands on me again. Why do you stay with him? I love him very much and besides if I leave him he can get an substantial amount of my money and I can't have that so I deal with him but if I have evidence of his infidelity I could divorce him and he gets nothing I guess he finds other women to take his frustrations out on since it's no longer me. I'm sorry about your wife but let me ask you a question, Will you be interested in working for me? I will pay you handsomely and pay for anything that you need. Yes I will, I need to get even with him for tearing my life apart. The next I knew my phone was ringing from a number I didn't recognize so I answered, it was the police department calling saying they needed to see me about my wife, I have to ma'am its important I arrived at the police station and they asked me did I know Theresa domenico, yes she's my wife did something happen to her, I'm sorry to inform you that she has committed suicide we found her in her car with an empty pill bottle and a message for you, no not my wife you have the wrong person, sir I need you to identify her body to see if it's her I arrived at the morgue and there was my beautiful Theresa she had killed herself I went numb not knowing what to do or say I just turned and left, Frank you don't have to tell me it's too hard for you, no Mrs. Taylor I want you to know everything so after I had a private service for her I decided I wanted to know what her letter said so I went back to the police department to talk to the detective. Detective Mendoza I want to see what was in the letter my wife left for me, Mr. Domenico I really don't think that's a good idea detective you don't understand I need to know please sir let me see it so he gave it to me it read " sweetheart I'm so sorry for what I've done to our marriage and I know you will never be able to forgive I can't even forgive myself for what I have done to you I'm sorry I was in love with him and I thought all the times he hit me was because he loved me so I hope you can find it in your heart to forgive me after I'm gone I love you". All she had to do was talk to me we could have fixed it. Mr. domenico I'm sorry for your lost would you like for us to peruse this matter of the beatings she received, no I'll take care of it thank detective. I left the station and went home I later received a phone call. I'm telling you all this Mrs. Taylor because the guy my wife was in love with the one who treated her so kind than treated her like a dog and was beating her, was Mr. Nesbit that's why I want you to be careful I don't want to see another woman hurt by this man. Mrs. Nesbit knew all of this that's why I decided to work for her you see he has all these high power attorneys that keeps getting him off now I'm on his track and determine to put an end to his manipulations and abusing of women. Oh frank I am so sorry you lost your wife but I don't understand I don't see him like that, I know you don't a lot of women don't some of the other women we had gotten to either was too afraid to testify or he paid to leave the country, I don't want to use you but I do want you to be careful. It's getting late frank if you like I have a guest room you can stay in, thank you but I think it's time for me to go home goodnight Mrs. Taylor goodnight frank and please call me Denese.

CHAPTER 14

When I went to bed I couldn't sleep I couldn't get what he told me out of my head I started to cry what have I gotten myself into with this man could he really be that dangerous. The morning came I was too tired to go to the office so I called in and decided to work from home if they needed me. My phone ranged and it was Alex, hello Alex how are you doing? Hello Denese what's wrong with you I was at your job and they said you didn't come in is everything alright, yes I was just feeling a little under the weather so I stayed home today, okay well I will be over to see you for lunch, Alex I don't know if today is a good day don't want you to catch what I have oh really like I said I'll see you for lunch and he hung up. That's the first time I heard him being demanding around 12:30 my buzzer ranged it was Alex. I let him in I had made us some grilled chicken salads which I knew he liked he came in and grabbed me in a bear hug and began kissing me I couldn't let him know what I had heard about him so I kissed him back this was man who was hard to resist any way I could see how a woman could get so wrapped up in him he had charm and charisma most of all he had a body to match how could someone so good looking and sexy be a woman beater. We sat down at the dining room table to eat our salads and have a glass of wine. Alex can I ask you a question, will you ever leave your wife for me? Denese once I get everything together we will be together forever I promise you that I just need you to be a little more patient with me can you do this for me, yes Alex I can but don't make me wait too long. What did you say to me? I said don't make me wait too long before I knew it he had slapped me crossed my face I was in shock What the hell is wrong with you why did you hit me like that, whenever I tell you something you don't question it I said we will be together as I turned and walked out of the kitchen he grabbed my arm and pulled me back into him, I'm sorry baby I had a rough day and I shouldn't have taking it out on you please forgive me he began kissing the bruise on my face and the tears began to roll down my face we left the kitchen I thought we were going to the couch but he pulled me into my bedroom and threw me on the bed Alex why are you being so rough with me today he snatched off my blouse and flipped me over and pulled up my skirt he rammed himself into me like never before and he whispered in my ear, this is mine all mine and I can and will take it whenever I want, I tried to move but he held me down and kept thrusting into me until I felt like I was being raped all I could do was lay there and cry when he finished his business I pulled myself up in bed and balled up like a baby and cried he went into the bathroom I never moved he got ready to go and leaned down to kiss me and left within in five minutes there was a knock on my door but I couldn't get up to answer it the next thing I knew my door swung open and I could hear frank calling my name but I couldn't answer he entered into my bedroom where he saw me curled up in the bed, denese are you alright I saw when Alex left like he was in a hurry I knew something was wrong do you want me to call the police or take you to the hospital, no Frank I will be alright, denese this is how it start with him if you don't put a stop to it it's only going to get worse, Frank I'm going to take a shower okay I'll go fix your door and wait for you after my shower I walked into the living room where I saw frank sitting on the couch with his head in his hands, frank I'm alright would you like a drink or something, no I'm fine I'm scared for you denese you have to be careful with him I sat down next to him and there was silence in the air for a long time frank turned to me to ask if I wanted to put an end to Alex's abusive behavior, what would I have to do frank first of all I must tell Mrs. Nesbit about you and show her the pictures from all the times yall were together than we would plan a scene and catch him in the act with you and have him arrested, what if he tries to hurt me don't worry denese I will be right here with you the whole time hiding and waiting for him to make a move I don't frank this could be dangerous and someone could get hurt, someone already got hurt go look in the mirror at your face I got up and went to the mirror my face was red and swollen frank rubbed the back of his hand across my face look what he's done to your beautiful face you can't allow this to go on he can really hurt you. We sat back down on the couch frank poured us another glass of wine I had turned my phone off because talking to Alex was not my plan for the night I guess what Alex had done to me took a toll on me frank was holding me in his arms the next thing I knew I woke up with him still holding me in his arms, oh frank I'm sorry I didn't mean to go to sleep on you its ok denese I didn't mind at all at least I know where you are and that you're safe frank I know you have to go I will get my locks on my door fix in the morning no denese I'm fine I can stay as long as you want me to. I looked into frank eyes they were filled with sympathy, love, and hatred, he leaned in to kiss me, it was so sensual I wanted to make love to him but after what Alex had done to me I was sore, frank I want you but I can't he hurt me, no denese don't be in no hurry to sleep with me I can wait until you're ready I want you all of you but in due time right now I just want to enjoy you I love talking to you and getting to know you and right now that's enough for me. Frank thank you for being here with me I guess if you wasn't following him you would have never known he hurt me we laid on the couch and just talked the rest of the night into morning frank got up and went into the kitchen I smelled something good he was cooking breakfast good morning frank smells good in here, I thought I would feed you before we both headed out for work, thank you that's thoughtful of you if you will excuse me I'm going to get ready for work I'll be back shortly, hurry back so your breakfast doesn't get cold, I will. I returned to the kitchen to have a seat with frank, looks good but you didn't have to cook vie already taking up all your time frank it's no problem denese I like spending time with you, I like spending time with you too frank once breakfast was over he headed over to the sink and started washing dishes frank you don't have to do that I can take care of those dishes later no I got them by the way how are you feeling I'm ok not sore like I was last night and my face is going down so I'm fine thanks for asking. I would like to take you somewhere later on if you don't have plans, well I'm going to try not to see Alex today I'll take care of that I'll tell Mrs. Nesbit to keep him occupied he won't even be able to call, so how about it can I see you after work, yes where do you want me to meet you know I will pick you up from work, what about my car well since I'm taking you to work I will pick you up also, you don't have to take me to work I will be fine I know that I want to take you to work and afterward we're going to have some fun, alright with me. I thought about frank all day he would send me text messages with smiley faces or just say hi and that he misses me he makes me feel like an high school girl when the work day was over he was outside standing by the passenger door waiting for me he, good evening Mrs. Taylor how was your day? Good evening Frank just fine and yours, it was good, so where are we headed Frank first we're going to the movies, okay fine with me lets go, what are we going to see it doesn't matter to me so we arrived at the movie theatre he came around to open my door I got out we walked hand in hand into the theatre once we got there I noticed a new movie out called bullet to the head with Sylvester Stallone, I want to see that frank do you mind no not at all whatever you want to see so he got our tickets we headed for the concession stand. I love movie popcorn we ordered a large tub of butter popcorn and some sodas and went to take our seats the movie was really good it was over we got ready to go and franks phone ranged it was Mrs. Nesbit saying that she needed to see him the next thing I knew my phone was going off and it was Alex saying he was coming to see me and for some strange reason I started to shake, that must be Alex cause his wife is saying she needs to see me so I guess he's left the house, so what are we going to do I will take you home and go see her I want you to play it cool and I will be back as soon as I can if you want that if not we will make him wait until he gets tired and go home. No frank it's good you can take me home I will be alright, are you sure denese yes frank its fine. We arrived at my place and I rushed in before Alex arrived at my house.

CHAPTER 15

Twenty minutes later the buzzer ranged it was Alex I let him in. hey baby I've missed you hey Alex missed you too, is that's the way you're going to greet me Alex I still feel the pain on my face and the pain you left in my body, baby I said I was sorry look I have something for you what is it Alex oh baby perk up I bought you a gift to show you how sorry I am for what I've done to you he took out this box and I opened it to my surprise it was a ruby and diamond ring about two carats oh Alex its beautiful I knew you would like it now come give your papi a kiss I leaned in and kissed him he started rubbing my breast he knew that would turn me on I could feel myself letting my guard down with him he started to undress me. Alex wait I can't I'm sorry my vagina is still in pain its ok baby I'll give you something else you like he unzipped my dress and let it fall to the floor than he unsnapped my bra and began sucking on my breast, oh Alex this feels so good he walked me into my bedroom and laid me on the bed he slid my panties off and started to take his clothes off he kissed all the way down until he reached my vagina and I knew once he started eating there he had me he sucked and he licked me until I could feel myself about to explode. Alex you're going to make me cum that's what I want to do cum for papi oh Alex I feel it Cuming he kept going the next thing I knew I had an explosive orgasm all over him he got up and came to me with his dick in his hands I knew I had to repay the favor since I was not going to fuck him, so I filled my mouth with him and I sucked him until he exploded which for some reason didn't take him long we decided to go take a shower together after our shower I headed for the kitchen to get something to drink when I came back to my room he was sitting on the bed wrapped in a towel from waist down I noticed my night stand drawer was open, looks like your gun been fired, yes it has I went to the gun range. Why are you snooping around? What are you going to do shoot me or something that's why you go to the range. No Alex I have to get ready for recertification so I went to practice, oh ok just making sure to see if I have to kill you before I let you kill me. Alex why would I want to kill you better yet why would you want to kill me, you belong only to me and if I catch you even thinking about another man than I will kill you, how can you say that you have a wife at home all I have is me so you're saying I can't have someone else in my life. No you can't have anyone but me now let's get some sleep. When morning came I was alone again I guess he had to get back to his wife's bed before she wakes up. My door buzzer was ringing and it was frank I let him, good morning Frank, good morning denese are you ok, yes I'm fine and you, yes I'm fine so did he hurt you? No he didn't but he did threating me, he told me if I get another man in my life he would kill me, so what am I supposed to do? I had a meeting with Mrs. Nesbit and told her you were ready to help me with him and she wants to meet you, why does she want to meet me? didn't you show her the pictures of me, no I didn't show her anything but I did tell her that he took you to Miami for your birthday, and how he really likes to spend money on you, well if she want all the gifts back she can have them after all it was her money that bought them all. No she's fine you keep them if you want them, so when are we going to meet her? In a few days she's lining up an important meeting he has to attend and we will go see her the room became quiet is there something on your mind frank, no not really come here Frank have a seat first of all let me ease your mind I didn't have sex with him at least none that required him to poke me, it's your body and he's your man you can do what you want to do, frank he hurt me and I told him I couldn't because I was still hurting. Denese you don't owe me an explanation I know he's your man and he require that you take care of him there is nothing I can do about that, Frank leaned in to kiss me and I gave in I really enjoy spending time with Frank. We decided to go to dinner after I got off work but what I really wanted to do was cook for him and just let him relax and help ease some of the pain in his heart I know I can't replace his wife and I don't want to but I want to l just want him to live again.

CHAPTER 16

Frank instead of going out to dinner, how about I just cook you dinner here at my place. Denese I don't want to take any chances while this man is able to be loose, it doesn't have to be here I do have another home in Colorado springs if you like we can go there for the weekend, that sounds nice but let's just hold off on leaving town for a minute. Ok than I will see you after work, you may see me before than if I know Alex is going to show up at your job so please be careful ok I will. We walked out of my place and went our separate ways. I went to work I knew there was going to be a Judges meeting I had to attend to so when Alex called I couldn't answer. I was interrupted by my assistant telling me I had an emergency phone call I excused myself I thought it was one of my boys but it wasn't, hello Mrs. Taylor here, why didn't you answer the phone Dens., Alex I'm in a meeting with the judges what's going on I called and you didn't answer, Alex I do have to work sometimes I'm getting ready to build a new court house so there are things I need to finish up with the judges and the officers now if you excuse me I will call you as soon as I'm finish. Ok Denese I will talk to you later. After the meeting was over I was headed back to my office when my assistant told me I had a visitor waiting for me in my office, as I entered my office Alex was sitting there behind my desk, hi Alex what are you doing here, I wanted to make sure you were really in a meeting and not out on a date I've noticed how good you've been looking lately and I know it's for another man, don't be silly Alex I put on makeup to cover the bruise you left on my face that's the only change I've made so now you don't trust me you have to come to my job to see if I'm really here. I'm sorry Denese I have to make sure nobody is messing with my property, your property I'm not a piece of real estate Alex I'm a human being so I'm not your property, for as long as I live you will be my property now I must go and I will see you later on tonight. When Alex left I sat down in my chair and wondered how did I get myself into this mess was I just looking for someone to love me after the way my husband treated me am I that desperate for a man what's going on in my life, it was about 6 o'clock I decided to call it a day and called for my car, by the time I was in my car my phone ranged it startled me I was hoping it wasn't Alex and it wasn't it was frank, hello Frank how are you, Denese you sound shaken up did that bastard hurt you when he came to see you today? No, how did you know he came to see me, did you forget I get paid to follow him and keep tabs on him, yes I forgot and no he didn't put his hands on me but he did shake me up talking about I'm his property and all, don't worry about him it will all be over soon I want to see you is it alright if I come by, I don't know frank he says he's coming over for dinner, its cool I will see you after he leaves, that will be fine. frank are you going to be nearby when he comes to see me, I plan to but I have to take care of some personal business first, ok I will see you later, until than be safe use your gun if you have to, ok I promise bye. I arrived home and headed for the kitchen to get dinner started I decided to make smother pork chops with some fried corn and green beans I haven't been grocery shopping since I've got back so I had to use what I had while the food was cooking I decided to take a shower and slip into something more comfortable just when the food was almost done the door buzzer rung it was Alex I let him in he came in and gave me a kiss, so how was your day Denese, it was good and yours mine was fine, dinner will be ready shortly so I went to set the table for the two of us to eat he went to the bathroom to freshen up when he came out everything was ready he took his seat while I fixed his plate and poured us a glass of red wine, at first there was silence in the air, denese are you still mad at me for hitting you? Yes I am, I told you I was sorry I've been under a lot of stress lately I didn't mean to take it out on you, I am so sorry please forgive me. Alex I'm mad and confused, what is there to be confused about, when you love someone you don't hurt them, so now what you doubting that I love you, Alex I just don't know you frighten me, it never use to be that way than you practically raped me and hurt me even more so that's why I'm confused, oh Denese come here sit on my lap I'm truly sorry I will never do that to you again I hope you can forgive me and he kissed me. After dinner we headed to the couch to watch some TV, Alex began rubbing on me, he would take his fingers and play with my nipples he knew that was one of my spot I started to relax and let my body give in to him, he lifted my t-shirt and pulled it over my head and began to kiss my neck until he worked his way down to my breast, he slowly unfasten my jeans and began to take them off once they were off he began kissing and licking my legs I was so turned on by this man how can he be an undercover monster he stood up and pulled me up with him I started to undress him I took off his shirt and began kissing his sexy chest down to the top of his pants I unzipped his pants and he slowly took them off he grabbed me by the hand and led me into the bedroom where I laid on the bed and watched him take off his boxers he got on his knees and spreaded my legs I knew what was coming I knew It was going to be over for me the way this man made love to me just melted all my insides and I forgot for a moment what he done to me, oh Alex this feels so good I can feel his tongue going in and out of my pussy while his fingers played with my clit, I knew I was about to cum, don't cum yet baby hold on I'm not ready for you to cum yet Alex I don't know how long I can hold it. He just kept going I could feel my insides wanting to burst all over him, Alex I'm Cumming I can't hold it he began to get faster with his tongue the next thing I knew I exploded he raised up and came and got on top of me I could feel the heat and passion between is he put his tongue in my mouth and his dick in my pussy it was nice and slow very sexual I just kept Cuming one orgasm after another when he finish he just laid there on top of me breathing hard I don't know what makes he think that he's a light weight but he's not Alex your heavy I can't breathe he laughed at me but he did move to lay next to me we laid there holding hands and breathing hard once our breathing slowed down he got up to shower I just laid in the bed his phone was vibrating being the nosey person that I am I looked at it and it said call from my baby, oh wow I wonder what he has me listed under it can't be his baby that's for sure he came back into the bedroom to retrieve his phone and take it with him while he showered I still laid in the bed when he was done he began to get dressed, Alex where are you going it's still early, I have somewhere to be so I'm leaving now, what you have to go home to your baby he looked at me but didn't say anything, I don't know how I could be so dumb and stupid when it comes to you I know you will never leave her for me the next thing I knew he had his hands around my throat, let me tell you something I will leave her when I'm good and ready so this fucked up attitude you got you better lose it and lose it fast, Alex I can't breathe he let go of my neck and finished getting dressed and again I found myself in tears but I didn't say anything to him I heard the door slammed and got up to check my neck and it had his palm print around it and was red. Denese what is wrong with you, why do you keep letting this man put his hands on you? I left the mirror and headed to the kitchen I stood there washing dishes and crying like a little bitch, if I kill him how much time will I get? if I claim self-defense I can't afford to go to jail, that's the thought I had in my mind, a few minutes later frank was calling my phone the first couple of times I wouldn't answer but I knew if I didn't he would bust down my door so the third time I answered. hi frank it's really not a good time right now I will call you later, denese don't hang up, frank I'm ok I will talk to you tomorrow and I hung up he called a few more times but I still didn't answer. I locked up my place and went to bed, the morning came I took my shower now my neck look black and blue so now I have to find something to put on that will cover up my marks around my neck. I found a nice dress that zipped up to my neck, it covered it really well and went to work, by the time I opened my apartment door frank was sitting at my door he jumped up, denese I was worried about you I couldn't sleep at all last night are you okay, yes frank I'm fine but I really do have to go I approached the elevator and he was right on my heels denese talk to me tell me what happen I know he did something to you what is it nothing frank please I have to go I rode the elevator by myself and got in my car and went on to work. I sat down at my desk and my assistant comes in with a delivery, roses let me guess who they're from just sit them over there and thank you Vicki for bringing them in. I read the card and once again it was Alex apologizing I put the card in my desk than my phone alerted me with a text it was frank, denese I know something happen and you don't want to talk about it but just know I am here for you whenever you need me the tears started to flow down my cheek I wiped them away I need to get to work I have a busy day ahead of me. How could a man who seem so sweet be so violent with women how could I be so stupid and fall for someone like this, by the time the day was done I took my phone out of my purse I had several missed calls and messages from frank but I was too embarrassed to talk to him he keeps telling me over and over to leave Alex alone but for some reason I cant. When I reached my car Alex was standing there waiting for me, hello beautiful how was your day? Fine Alex what are you doing here you come to apologize some more, denese you know I don't mean to hurt you but you like to provoke me all you have to do is be my woman and do what I say without any lip service behind it or worry about my wife, oh is that all I need to get in my car I have some errands I need to take care of so if you will please excuse me, what errands I have plans for us tonight, plans like what Alex, we have dinner reservations and a night of dancing, Alex I'm tired I need to go to the store and go home and get ready for work tomorrow, you can go home after dinner so either you follow me to the restaurant or get in my car, I will drive myself thank you. I got in my car and followed him through the parking garage as we were leaving I saw franks car parked on the side of another car so I knew I would be safe because he will be following Alex. As we approached the restaurant I pulled up in valet behind Alex to have my car parked he grabbed me by the hand as we entered into the restaurant it was such a beautiful place as the waiter escorted us to our table, Alex had the nerve to ask me what's wrong, nothing Alex I'm fine as we sat he ordered a bottle of champagne, what are you celebrating Alex, we are celebrating us it's been six wonderful months since we've met, in my mind the first three was wonderful but these last three has been hell on wheels, oh really you remembered that I'm shocked most men don't remember things like that, well I'm not most men I remember everything about you since I've met you, the waiter poured us each a glass of the bubbly, I have something for you on this six month anniversary denese, happy anniversary baby I love you he took out a box from Jared jewelers my eyes opened wide because they have some of the best jewelry in the world, I opened the box and it was beautiful diamond necklace, Alex thank you so much its really beautiful but I can't except it, why can't you except it denese, Alex you keep hurting me than you want to act like nothing has happened and shower me with flowers and diamonds after you do, I don't really know what to think anymore, denese I don't want to hurt you at all you just make me so angry at times well is it that your wife makes you angry and you take it out on me, sometimes she makes me angry but most of the times when you don't do as you are told or if you keep mouthing off you make me angry and if you don't except my gift I will be very angry, well if it means that you won't hit me I will except. We continued with our dinner our conversation was minimum at best the restaurant had a dance floor and they began to play Freddie Jackson I knew Alex had something to do with that, may I have this dance denese, sure you can Alex you know I love this man and could dance to him all night and it seemed like all night too because every song was him. After we finished dancing and headed back to the table, I noticed the waiter placing our desert on the table my second favorite, tiramisu, Alex I guess you thought of everything, I told you I remember everything you've ever said to me about your likes and dislikes I ate my desert he paid the check and we headed to the door. We both waited for our cars at the valet station, denese it's too late for you to go to the store so I'm headed to your house for a night cap, ok Alex I'll do my grocery shopping tomorrow, we'll see what tomorrow holds baby we both got into our car and pulled off, my phone ranged it was frank I decided to answer hi frank I didn't mean to ignore you I'm sorry for that, denese I worry about you that's why I try and keep in touch I know he hurts you and now he's hurting you on a daily basis, when are you going to let him go, if I do I'm scared he will come back for revenge I don't know how to let him go, I think I really love him frank, the tears started to roll down my face, denese listen to me I will protect you I will not let this maniac kill you or you kill yourself like my wife did do you hear what I'm saying to you I will kill him before I let that happen, frank I got to go we are about to turn into my apartment complex I need to clean my face before he sees me, denese wait I hung up instantly. We walked into my place I immediately took my stilettos off my shoes are not made to be worn for twelve hours, Alex went to the kitchen I went into my bathroom to take my clothes off and slip on some sweat pants and tank top. I came out the bathroom Alex was sitting on the couch with two glasses of wine, he had the music playing soft and low and a few candles lit, here you go baby come sit and have a drink with me ok I sat down next to Alex we toasted each other and I placed my glass on the table, denese what's wrong you are so quiet do you want to talk about something? No Alex I'm fine I don't want to ask any questions I'm afraid you might get angry at me and my body really can't afford any new bruises. Denese I'm sorry for messing up your body but if you want to talk I promise not to get angry and hit you, no I'm fine Alex I'm going to take a shower if you don't mind I'm tired, go ahead I will be here when you get back, I went into the bathroom and took my clothes back off and while standing in the mirror I was looking at my body, I had another hand print around my neck, both of my arms were bruised, I had marks on my thighs and on my back I began to cry, I never saw Alex come in the bathroom but he was standing behind me he began kissing my shoulders and my back than he worked his way back up to my neck, he turned me around to face him and started wiping the tears from my face, baby don't cry I'm so sorry I promise I will never hit you again please forgive me, the tears started to roll down his face and I was sure he meant what he said. He grabbed me in a bear hug and just held me in silence I let go to enter into the shower he took off his clothes and stepped into the shower with me, Alex began to kiss me and it was so passionate I felt warmth in my body like I did the first time we kissed he began moving down my body with his tongue I could feel the heat between us I started to tingle all over my body I wanted this man so much and he knew he had a hold on me. We began to make love in the shower he ate my pussy so good I swear I had four to five orgasm, once he was finished we headed to the bed he laid on his back and I climbed him and rode him until the bed couldn't take no more I continue to cum for this man over and over I thought we were finished didn't think I had nothing else left in me but when I laid on my back he began playing with my nipples and they stood up at attention I began to tingle again, his fingers were so soft on my breast he pulled my nipples so hard that it didn't hurt just turned me on more than he climbed on me and began to kiss my soft lips even his tongue is soft and sweet we kissed so passionately for a while than he slid his dick into me and went to town he always knew where my g-spot was he manage to hit it every time no matter whether it was from the back or the front I continue to cum a few more times, by than I am totally exhausted and we I laid there in his arms for the night and we had a wonderful conversation I thought I was back in Miami that's how good it was, I fell asleep there feeling all good and tired but this time when I woke up he was still there so I wondered why, did his wife put him out or something or did he leave her for me I had this big smile on my face, he got up and went into the bathroom I watched him as he passed by, Alex do you want some breakfast, no you stay there I will make you breakfast call your assistant and tell her you're not coming in today, why I need to read over these contracts and make some calls, you can do that from home have her to messenger the contracts to you and send you the phone numbers of all the people you need to call, what about your job Alex you don't have to go in, no I'll take my meetings on the phone I'm going to spend the whole day with, really you are ok I will call Vicki and let her know I won't be in today. Alex called his office to advise them he would not be in and to clear his schedule he will take his important meetings on his cell phone. I was really shocked at this sudden change in him I wonder what his wife has to say about this, I received a text message on my phone from frank it says, hi denese I know Alex is with you Mrs. Nesbit is out of town for a few days but I will be here as long as he's in there with you. I didn't have a chance to respond to him Alex walked in, now I know why he's spending time with me his wife is out of town if I ask him about his wife it may trigger him and I don't want to be hit on today so I will just keep my mouth closed and enjoy the day. Hey babe do you want to go out on the town for a while, Alex we both have work to do but I do need to go to the grocery store and some other stores sometime today, ok we can do that I'll take you where you need to go, why thank you that's very sweet of you I'll go get dressed so we can go out early I went to out on a pair of jeans my tight ones that shows all my curves and a tank top to show my beautiful cleavage and my gym shoes. Alex had brought in an overnight bag so he put on a pair of jeans and a t-shirt that shows off his six pack which by the way is very sexy we headed out the door he decided to drive my car I believe it was because I have tinted windows and he didn't want to be recognize in case some of his wife's friends saw him, we drove out of the city to go shopping which was really crazy it was an half hour out but our first stop was a nice little bistro to get something to eat, Alex why are we so far away from home shopping in the city would be much easier don't you think, baby I just want to take you someplace else we are always in the city so just let me drive and you sit back and enjoy the ride, we sat down and he ordered for me a glass of wine and him a jack and coke we sat in out booth and just talked it was falling for him all over again after some time had passed I decided to order me some food so I ordered lasagna and a salad Alex didn't order anything he said he will just share my food, so Alex what do you have plan for us today, well since you must know we're going to do some shopping maybe catch a movie if its ok with you, yes it will fine with me after we finished eating we headed to Saks fifth avenue and Niemen Marcus and we shopped and had fun after shopping we went to the movie theatre I don't even know what's playing and I really don't think we cared we got popcorn and candy and sat down to watch the show, it turned out to be anew movie that had just came out called "snitch" with the rock Alex knew I had a secret crush on the rock and he was starring in it as the lights got dim Alex put his hand on my leg and began to rub, denese I want you, Alex you always want me, I do but I want to play with you right here and now he unfasten my jeans I could feel his fingers in my panties traveling and playing with my clit he was turning me on I couldn't concentrate on the movie, Alex people are sitting next to us what are you doing, if you don't scream they will never know what we are doing, I could feel myself letting my body move to the movement of his fingers, I took my free hand and unzipped his jeans and started to rub his penis, his bulge was hard so I put my hand in his underwear and I stroked him and stroked him he was moaning where as I can only hear him here we are to grown ass people acting like teenagers in a movie theatre he was finger fucking me and I was palm fucking him and it felt good I could feel myself about to cum and I knew he was to be released at the same time, dam you Alex you made me wet my pants, well I guess we both wet he leaned in and kissed me, I could not even tell you what happen on the movie so I guess I'll have to come back and see it another time without Alex we decided to go ahead and leave we didn't know what was going on anyway we drove home holding hands and smiling at each other, when we reached the parking garage I heard his phone vibrating, I have to take this please excuse me, I was going to get out of the car so he can talk but he grabbed my hand for me to stay, I could tell it was his wife calling, yes I took care of all the important things that had to be taking care of today, ok have a safe flight back and I will see you tomorrow ok goodbye, he didn't say I love you to her, come on baby lets go inside I exited the car with a big smile on my face maybe he is going to leave her for me. Once in the apartment he pulled me into him, thank you for a wonderful day Mrs. Taylor, you're welcome Mr. Nesbit. I went to put my bags in the room still have no groceries Mr. Nesbit, I'm sorry baby we will get them tomorrow I promised, Alex went into the bathroom I could hear the water running in the tub, my phone alerted me of a text message, hi Mrs. Taylor I see you had a full day looks like you were having fun but I still remind you to please be careful I'm still here I responded to him, thanks frank but don't you need to get some sleep I will be fine, he responded back as long as that asshoe is with you I won't sleep so please be careful. I decided not to respond back I heard Alex calling my name to come get into the tub with him I put the phone down and headed to the bathroom. The music was playing over the intercom system, baby I want you to give me a show, you want me to do what, give me a strip show let me see what you're working with, Alex are you serious, yes I'm serious the music playing the lights are dim take your hair down and show daddy what you can do. I started moving to the music and slowly undressing I was giving him a strip tease show like never before he was all turned on I could see through the water in the tub how excited he was getting and I started to take off my panties and turned my ass toward him and began to shake it in his face he was excited he spanked my ass over and over than he pulled me into the water on his lap, baby you are so sexy I can just eat you up, well as soon as we get out of this tub I want you to do just that eat me up, I will baby lets bathe so we can get out. We got out I headed to the bedroom to lotion up my body and put on something sexy he followed me I got into my bed waiting for him, denese I have something for you that I ordered for you, what is it I took a box out of the bag and it was the newest toy from 'bedroom kandi" called happiness and joy and it brings a lot of joy I couldn't wait to use it. Alex thank you but what made you buy this I thought you were all the dick I needed? Denese I know you like vibrators you a drawer full of them and I thought you would like this yes Alex I do I mean I like my vibrators and I like this, well come on over here and show papi how you use it. I put the batteries in and turned it to full power I played with myself and I swear the power this thing has had me about to explode Alex watched me as I pleasured myself and he was as hard as a brick I continued to cum every time I would put the penis part in me and the vibrator part on my clit I almost wore myself out. Now denese save some of that for me come get it baby its hot and really wet waiting for you to stick it in I moved my toy to the side of the bed and Alex climbed on top of me, oh denese you are so wet I might cum in a minute, Alex that's not funny I don't need a minute man and he continued to pound in me and it felt so good all I could do was scream and release than Alex released, oh my what powerful sex we have I was exhausted and tired all I wanted to do was go to sleep.

CHAPTER 17

The morning came and Alex was gone, my buzzer rung I put on my robe and went to answer the door. Hi frank have you been here all night? Yes denese I was are you alright? Yes I'm fine, frank I know you are worried about me but I think Alex and I are going to be fine he was like a different person last night, the man I first met about six months ago, listen denese that's how he works my wife was not the only woman he's done this to love them, beat them, and love them again than beat them it's his pattern I care what happens to you and I don't want to see you hurt by him, I know your husband hurt you maybe not physically but emotionally denese you deserve so much better someone to love you for who you are and makes you happy not hurt you in any kind of way, I guess that's you frank, denese whether it's me or another man you deserve better. Alex is gone to be with his wife and probably to clean himself up like he hasn't done anything while she was gone, frank I need to get ready for work thank you for being concerned about me but I will fine, ok denese I have to go take care of yourself and watch that man and most of all don't trust anything that he says to you do we understand each other, yes frank I got you. Frank left and I began to get ready for work when my phone ranged this time it was my estrange husband, what do he want, I answered the phone yes may I help you, denese I need to see you can we meet this week for dinner I need to talk to you, why what do you have to say to me in person that you can't say over the phone, please I want to do this in person please can we meet this Friday please for dinner, ok I'll see you Friday after work text me the information as to where you want to do this. Could this morning get any more busier before I get to work I hurried up and got dressed before anymore distractions come about and left I arrived at work and my assistant Vicki was waiting for me with a cup of coffee, Vicki I might need a few cups this morning so keep the coffee pot full. I was busy I didn't even notice what time it was I never even stopped for lunch it was already 3pm my assistant kept the coffee coming I made all my phone calls took all my meetings that I had missed the day before but we were on point. Vicki you can call it a day go home early we're not doing any more work today, thank you Mrs. Taylor I will see you tomorrow, ok have a good evening. After Vicki left I decided to leave also I still needed to go grocery shopping I locked the office and headed to the market, when I arrived home frank was in the parking garage in his car crying, frank are you alright, what's wrong, I opened his car door to help him get out his car come on frank lets go in my place I gathered up my groceries and he helped we headed to the elevator and went upstairs, frank still hasn't said anything to me I opened the apartment door we went in he took his bags to the kitchen placed them on the counter and left out he was headed back to the door, frank wait don't leave sit down and talk to me please I want to know what's wrong, today is my wife's birthday and she's not here to celebrate all because of your man, frank I am so sorry I really didn't know what else to say I just put my arms around him and held him without saying anything after a while I asked him if he would like a drink, yes please you have something other than wine, of course I do what do you have a taste for, how about some vodka and cranberry if you have it, yes I have it, have you eaten anything today? I don't think so well I will fix you something to eat, nothing heavy please I do appreciate it, thank you so much, it's no problem here is your drink I will fix us something to eat, I walked into the kitchen frank followed me, frank why don't you just lay down on the couch until I finish you look really tired, no denese I want to be in here with you I'm ok just had a bad moment I know they say time will make it easier but right now living day to day is hard for me, frank do you believe in god and the power of prayer? I don't know why you ask frank I've always been a church girl I have the world's greatest pastor and he always teach us the bible and the things

I have gone through and still go through I learned that god puts us through a test to let us know who is and he doesn't give us more than we can bear, the devil have a lot of temptations out here and we have to be strong enough to try and fight him off what I'm trying to say is that the devil tempted your wife and she fell for it that's not your fault but now he wants you to lean and depend on him so that he can help you through this I know the anger in you is overwhelming and has taking control of your mind but I hope you lean on him and let him help you get your life back, well once this man is behind bars and suffer for all the things he has done to these women the anger will remain. Ok frank I want you to sit here and eat with me I made us an omelet I hope you don't mind this is what I really had a taste for, no this is great well its sausage and cheese and here is your toast so put your drink to the side and drink this orange juice, ha-ha you should have put the vodka in the orange juice, you are funny here eat up after we finished eating we headed back into the living room to have a seat on the couch, would you like to watch TV or listen to some music, it doesn't matter I just want to sit here with you if you don't mind, no I don't mind let me tell you about a phone call I received today from my husband, he said he needs to see me, and what did you say? I said yes we're going to meet on Friday for dinner, what do you think he wants? I don't know maybe he's ready to divorce me or something I don't know but it will be nice to see him it's been a long time since we saw each other and it will be good to let him see he didn't break me and also see how good I look and what he's missing. Denese now you're the one funny but you do have a point you do look good, thank you. We sat there and talked for hours it was midnight. Denese I must go I've taking up too much of your time already, frank you don't have to leave you can stay if you like I really enjoy your company and we really have good conversations and it feels good to have someone to laugh with, denese you could have this all the time if you let me, frank you know I'm seeing Alex, well denese I wish it was me you were seeing I think you are very special and I'm not saying that to get into your panties either it's not about sex you have something in you that makes you sexy inside and out, I leaned in to give him a kiss and he pulled back, frank what's wrong, no denese I do want you but all of you not half of you and I know you love Alex or to me your just blinded by him but I don't think this is a good idea while you're involved with him, I understand frank I'm sorry don't be wanted you since the first day I laid eyes on you but I promise you nis when he breaks your heart I will be here for you until than we will maintain our friendship. Now I must be leaving before I change my mind, thank you for the shoulder to cry on, you are so welcome please don't be a stranger.

CHAPTER 18

The next day was another work day but there wasn't a lot of things to do except go over my employees personnel files I needed to do some promotions and some interviews for the new courthouse I was opening up I needed to hire more officers for the building more officers to protect the judges so that's what I'm going to spend the next few months doing, by the end of the day I noticed that frank or Alex had called. When I left work I made a few stops and headed home, when I arrived in my parking garage I saw Alex car I pulled beside him and got out. Hi Alex how was your day? Fine and you, just great I haven't heard from you today, I was busy all day what about you, was you busy today, yes I was what's wrong are you trying to say something to me, no just curious come on lets go up. We got into the apartment Alex went into the kitchen to make him a drink Alex are you sure you're alright, you're very quiet, I told you I was fine, well I wanted to talk to you but I don't think it's a good time oh baby you can tell me anything I'm sorry I'm just a little distracted that's all, so what do you want to talk about, I received a phone call from my ex he says he needs to talk to me, what about, I don't know he didn't say maybe we're going to finally discuss our divorce or maybe it's about the kids I don't know yet but I plan on seeing him tomorrow or Saturday, well I think I should be there when you see him, no I'm not ready for that yet, what you mean you not ready to let him see your man, Alex do you let me go with you to see your wife I think not, I'm not separated from my wife, yeah I know (slap) why the hell did you just slap me in my face Alex what the hell is wrong with you, so you think you can go see him and fuck him and I shouldn't care, who the hell said anything about fucking him, you got a lot of nerve you sleep with your wife just about every night I know you got to be fucking her and I don't say shit so if I was fucking someone you shouldn't have nothing to say. The next thing I knew this man was on top of me with his hands around my neck and yelling at me than hitting me in my face like he has lost his mind, once again I was black and blue, Alex get out of my house I'm tired of being your punching bag I want you to leave now, he hesitated and by this time I had had enough, I went to my night stand to retrieve my gun he leaped across the bed and grabbed me, oh you think you're going to shoot me I will kill you first so I suggest you think twice about that he turned and left, I decided to call frank now it was time to put this man behind bars before he kills me but before I could call he was knocking on my door, I opened the door he was in a rage, denese that's enough it's time for you to put a stop to this before he kills you, all I wanted frank to do was hold me he went into the bathroom to get a wash cloth to clean my face, frank I just want to lay down in my bed right now, he took me to my room I laid there in a fetal position and he laid with me, I felt safe with his arms around me, denese talk to me what do you want to do, please I'm here to help you talk to me, but I didn't say anything I just knew I wasn't going to be going out the house tomorrow looking like this, my lip was busted my eyes were black my neck was bruised my arms were sore, I just wanted to stay where I was with the person I was with, I end up texting my ex to tell him I couldn't meet him I would have to wait until the following weekend, I stayed home from work the following day I didn't want Alex to know I was home so I had my sister Diane to come get my car, Alex was blowing up my phone with his calling and texting talking about how sorry he was, but I wouldn't respond to him, he was coming by my apartment but I never would make a sound so that he wouldn't know I was there, frank stayed with me all day and all night I actually stayed in all weekend and he stayed with me we really had a good time in spite of what happen and it didn't involve sex.

CHAPTER 19

Monday morning came I had concierge to get me a car so I could go to work and my sister would bring my car this afternoon or I would go over there and pick it up, I got to work and went right into it, Alex was calling but I told Vicki to tell him I was in meetings and could not be disturb. That Saturday morning frank was still in my apartment I was smelling food so I got up and he was making breakfast and coffee for me, I went into the kitchen, oh no denese I want you to stay in bed I'll bring your food to you, oh frank how sweet, but I'm ok I can sit here in the kitchen well at least go into the living room and sit on the couch please so I went because I didn't feel up to arguing and besides my body was very sore, frank came in with my breakfast and placed it on the table in front of me, frank it smells good but I don't really feel hungry, its ok but you need to eat to build up your strength so please try to eat a little something so I did actually I ate almost all of it, frank I'm going to take a shower I will be back, ok I'll clean up my mess in the kitchen, I headed to the bathroom and turned on the water when I undressed I looked at my body and began to cry I stepped into the shower while washing my body my arms felt so heavy I couldn't life them, like I wanted to but then I felt a hand on me, its ok denese I will help you, frank grabbed the sponge from my hand and began to wash me he never said anything he washed my front than my back parts when he was done and I rinsed off he turned off the water and help me step out the shower he took me into my room and helped me put on a pair of pajamas I didn't want him to see me like this but it was unavoidable at this point I laid in my bed he pulled the covers up on me, sleep denese I will be here when you wake up, frank could you stay lay down with me please, he climbed into bed and put my head under his arm, denese you want to talk about it, frank I don't understand why I continue to let men abuse me and treat me like shit what's wrong with me how could I continue to fall for the wrong person I thought when I was married I had the perfect life but come to find out I didn't, I thought we were so happy together but I was a fool than don't get me wrong the first fifteen years was really good he always put me first made me feel special all the time we use to take these wonderful vacations always went to dinner or we cook for each other and the sex was wonderful but as the years started to pass I notice a change in him, he was always consume with my best friend whom I treated like my family whatever they wanted he was Johnny on the spot I started to complain about it but he didn't care he did what he wanted to do no matter how I felt about it but things got crazy he was in the hotel with her he was taking her out to dinner while I laid up in the hospital from surgery he would lie and say he was going to the store and for twelve hours he would be gone and wouldn't answer his cell phone he was disappearing all the time so one day I was sick and told him I needed some laundry detergent he said ok I'll pick you up some he left about three in the afternoon but as time went by I kept calling and he wouldn't answer so I noticed that my car keys were gone so I guess he took them so I wouldn't follow him but that didn't stop me I had friends with cars who I knew would come pick me up and my friend did about 2 in the morning I went on the hunt and I kind of knew where to go and true enough he was at my best friend's house I was steaming I had my knife and my gun I was just gone flat out kill them both but my friend wouldn't let me get out the car she drove off back to the house I said ok this the game how want to play than we will play together I went to work and I knew this liked me so I gave in to him so one day I took him up on his offer to go out to lunch so I found myself going to lunch with him almost every day my husband was still ignoring me and still fucking around with my best friend and some other girls I knew so I let him go right ahead so I started to disappear like him but I wasn't good at him and he had followed me so when I got home from work he was waiting for me and he started talking all kind of shit about where I was and who I was with, you got a lot of nerve out here fucking everything that has a pussy and you want to talk about me and call me a hoe and a bitch fuck you he stated he didn't want me anyway he was only with me because of the kids but now our kids was grown and on their own, oh really that's all I was good for was taking care of the kids and cleaning the house and cooking and let's not forget paying bills cause you made sure every dime of my check went to pay bills so that I would be broke and have to ask you for money and watch you laugh in my face, so I guess you wanted someone smaller than me now I guess you are tired of me, I watched how you were always on the computer watching porn how you would go to the video store and buy porn how you would to the novelty store to buy the same kind of vibrators for someone else like the ones we used and you know what I'm tired I will not take any more of your shit so as time went on he came and went there was hardly any talking between us so I got fed up and decided to leave him and I did, how could I be so stupid and not see the signs of him fucking around on me long before I did he had been doing it so long before I knew it he meant everything to me my lifeline but after I went through a brief dark stage in my life I had hit the lotto for quite a bit of money where as I could own my business I always worked in the court system and loved my job so I bought the building and revamped the whole thing I did a lot of firing and hiring and was determine to get a life for myself so I threw myself into my work and I joined a gym to get my body back and my soul I always went to church but church wasn't always in me so when I learned to put my trust in him and give him my time things started to work out for me, here I am one of the richest girls in America dealing with a married man who likes to beat on me so tell me frank what's wrong with me why can't I get a single man to love me and me only, first of denese there is nothing wrong with you, you attract the wrong guys and they mean you no good they take advantage of you when they see how vulnerable you are but what you need to do is go back to god and ask him to forgive you than you meet with your husband let him see what he's missed out on and you ask him for forgiveness you need to do that for yourself not for him you need to get your life back in tact so you can enjoy it fully but most of all get back into church they way you use to be and let me put this man in jail for you things will work out I know you have the faith go back to praying and believing denese you know how talk to god with a sincere heart let him work it out for you and he will bless you with the right kind of man, how do you know so much frank, me and my wife use to go to church we were active members but we let our job interfere and we started hanging out with friends and one thing led to another and we got lost in ourselves, we had talked about our lives well into the morning, we finally fell asleep I was still in his arms when I woke up. I wanted to go to church but didn't because my body was still a little bruised and sore so we decided to stay in frank was still there he did run home for a minute to get some changing clothes and came back and we continue to talk it was so great just to talk to someone and laugh and joke and just enjoy the company. As the day went on we watched movies and listen to music I just felt good being with him but was he a wolf in sheep's clothing I wondered, later that afternoon frank asked me if I wanted to leave the house and go out for a while I was really hesitate about going but why not I deserve a life for myself and to be happy so we got dressed and headed out. First we went to the park someplace I haven't been in a long time we were like kids he pushed me on the swings and we walked around playing in the grass, we saw an ice cream truck, let's get some ice cream denese, sure why not lets go so we raced to the truck, than we left the park and went to get something to eat, frank I am really having a good time thank you so much for bringing me out, denese you deserve this and more are you ready to go home, yes I'm ready so I can get ready for work tomorrow back to the drawing board what are you going to do tomorrow frank, well its back to following Mr. Nesbit whenever he and his wife gets back she will let me know when they land, oh ok I guess he's going to try and contact me tomorrow when he gets back, I'm sure he will I plan on meeting with his wife so we can get the ball rolling on him and find out what the plan will be, so how involve do I have to be in order for you to catch him, denese we don't have to talk about that right now let's just enjoy the rest of the evening ok honey, ok frank I have been having a good weekend and don't want to talk about him right now. Ok it was Sunday so I decided to make us a nice dinner and stay in to watch the game, frank seem to be having a better day and I was happy I was in the kitchen preparing dinner and he walked in, denese do you need any help? No frank I'm good but thanks for asking, you're welcome well I'll just sit here and watch you, ok well let me ask you a serious question frank, go ahead I'm listening, as many times as you've seen me naked and have laid in the bed with me, how come you've never tried anything with me, frank got out of his chair and came around where I was at the counter, denese I really like you not for sex because of who you are, you are a very sweet and loving person with so much to offer a person guys like to take advantage of and I'm not that kind of person I like you for you not for what's between your legs denese and I want you but all of you not bits and pieces, do you understand so until I think you're ready to give yourself to me I'll continue to take cold showers(laughing) I'll keep holding you in my arms until I think you're ready to give yourself to me and denese you are worth waiting for don't let any man fool you into thinking you're not, well frank is it ok for me to kiss you, he leaned in and dam it was so passionate yet so lovely I could feel the heat in this man now I need a cold shower. After I finish cooking we got ready for to sit down and have dinner, there was a knock on my door frank looked out the peep hole it was a delivery so he answered the door with his hand on his gun as usual, I have a delivery for denese Taylor I'll take it thank you than frank tipped the delivery boy and sent him on his way, here denese these are for you I'm sure you know who they are from apologizing again I betcha, true enough they were from Alex saying he's sorry again I just sat them in the kitchen me and frank were in the dining room about to eat dinner, frank are you ok yes denese I'm fine I will be glad when we get rid of him that's all, I know frank but let's not it mess up our evening please, frank lit the candles on the table and I fixed us both a plate and he poured us some wine, dam denese who taught you how to cook like this, my aunt who passed away taught me well she's done a dam good job this food is delicious, why thank you haven't had a compliment like that about my food in a very long time so I'm glad you are enjoying it, she was like my mother I was with her all the time and when my parents divorced I moved in with her and my uncle, I had the greatest uncle in the world he was very protectant of me and I was of him, we use to lie down in bed and he would show me how to crochet and I did it too he would make sure I had yarn when I got of school so I could knit something we would eat together and sing the blues I loved him so much but he passed away and left me I thought I was going to die when that happen than it was me and my aunt and as I got older and she was cooking she would have me in the kitchen she would say, get your ass over here and learn how to cook this, I would laugh but she made sure I knew how to do it and how to season it but anyway she passed away and left me back in 1998 and I miss her every day especially around her birthday cause we use to party for her birthday no matter whether it was raining snowing cold hot we didn't get care we would get something to drink and cook some food and just have a good time she taught me how to play cards especially spades and poker she would have these card parties and I would be the waitress and serve food and drinks and when people start to get drunk my tips would get bigger and she would say go get them denese make that money she cooked all the time and we just had fun with her she was the brick that held our family together and I miss her so much and her husband he was great. We continued with our meal and conversation, as the day went along we ordered some movies off Netflix and I made some popcorn for us to eat I never did put on any clothes I was just so cozy and comfortable with him after our movies we noticed how late it was getting, denese I want to talk to you about Alex if you don't mind, no go ahead we can talk about him I don't want you to see him anymore I want to stay away from him can you do that, yes frank I think I can but I need to talk to him to let him know I don't want to see him anymore well when you do I want to be here with you I really think when you tell him he's going to be even more violent with you and I don't want him to hurt you cause I might kill him, I know frank and it's going to be rough on the both of us I love him I just want him to stop hitting on me, listen denese there is a lot more out there than being with a man who abuse you I don't understand why some women think that a man could only love them if he's hitting on them and treating them like shit you are a good person and deserve to be happy with someone who will love you not your money not for what's between your legs but you I've spent over six months with you and I haven't had sex with you and that's because I know you're more than that I watched you let him hurt you and try and hide from him and the world because of the bruises I watched you cry about him and your husband now it's time for you to get your life back from the both of them so first you go and have this meeting with your husband and second you have your meeting with Alex and end them both and then find denese back get her back to the woman she's supposed to be and the most important thing you get yourself back in love with god and let him help you through this I will be here if you need me and if you want me but you have to take care of your issues first I'm not trying to be mean but its time, denese I really like you, you have stirred up some feelings in me that I had lost and I like it but whether it's me or someone else be loved by somebody who wants to love you the right way. Frank thank you for everything and yes it's time for me to do all that and I really like you too, so many times I wanted you to make love to me and you wouldn't touch me, denese I don't want you to think that's all I want from you cause it's not, I know that now frank and I really do appreciate the fact that's not all you want from me, don't get me wrong it's been hell on me cause I really want to make love to you and then fuck your brains out but I know you're not ready for me and I understand, frank I'm going to call my husband tomorrow and meet with him than I will meet with Alex and let them both go, and when you do I will be here for you denese I better go now, no frank please don't go stay with me I promise I won't bite, no denese I think I should go I will see you soon come lock the door as we walked to the door he turned around and gave me a kiss on my cheek, bye denese, goodbye frank have a good night oh I plan to I will dream only of you goodbye.

CHAPTER 20

Frank left I headed to the bathroom for a nice cool shower, it was morning and I was feeling good the first thing I had to do was get on my knees and pray and I did I got ready for work when my phone alerted me of a text message, it was frank good morning beautiful hope your night was good thank you for a lovely weekend have a beautiful day see ya soon, I responded to him by saying yes my night was beautiful I had a great time this weekend with you as well I hope you do see me soon. I got to work a met with the construction guys and everything was going according to the plans I called my husband and told him I needed to see him so we schedule to meet that Friday after work I called my attorney and told him to go ahead with the divorce papers I needed them by Friday nothing fancy just your average divorce papers cause there was nothing for us to fight over our kids were grown and married, our house was paid for so if he sells I get half the money anyway and the millions I have now came after we separated and I set it up where he couldn't get any of it anyway not unless I wanted to give him some we didn't have any joint accounts and the cars were his anyway I had lost everything I had that was in my name and since he didn't help me keep my things I have no reason to give him anything I have so there was really nothing we need to fight over. Later that day Alex called to say he had a business meeting out of town and will be back Saturday, ok Alex I will see you when you get back, in the back of my mind I figure it was another woman he was seeing anyway and was probably taking her out of town with him but I was having such a good day my thoughts were not going to get in my way today. My assistant Vicki came into my office and said I had a visitor and he carrying the most beautiful bouquet of flowers ever, who is it Vicki, he told me not to say just said to let you know the weekend was here, is there anything you want to tell me Mrs. Taylor that I missed, no Vicki show him in and hold my calls please thank you, I had the biggest smile on my face like a child in a candy store, he came into my office and dam he was looking good. Hi frank what a surprise I didn't expect to see you today, hello denese I couldn't go all day and not see you, have a seat please, I sat in the chair next to him in my office instead of my desk chair, so what's going on frank are you alright, yes I am but I do need to ask you a question, Mrs. Nesbit informed me that Alex brought two airline tickets for Vegas and I was wondering where you going with him, no frank it's not me I will be here with you but don't you have to go and take pictures or something, no I will send my assistant to follow him I would like to stay here with you if you don't mind, no I don't mind at all when is he going, in a few days, oh ok that's nice, you don't seem upset denese, I'm not I'm fine with him seeing someone else its time I cut all my ties with him anyway and take my life back and move on, you Mrs. Taylor I like the sound of that, and lately frank you have been a little more happy and I like to keep it that way, it's because of you denese, you have helped me come out of my depress stage a lot and I'm beginning to get some feeling back in my body and some love in my heart instead of all this anger and hate, don't get me wrong I still want him to pay for what he's done to you and my wife and I intend to make sure that happens. I understand frank and it's really nice to see you a lot calmer these days I really like that, do you have any plans when you get off work today? None that comes to mind what do you want to do? I figure we can go out for a little while and have a few drinks and dance the night away, that sounds really nice frank I would like that very much, ok until than I will see you later I will call you with the game plan and times ok I want to go home and shower and change so I'll probably leave early. He leaned in and to kiss me and it was really nice, see you later Mrs. Taylor and he left my office for a minute I just sat there and thought about him and what I would like to do to him if giving the chance Vicki walked in I had this big grin on my face, I see someone is very taking with this man, yes Vicki I am he's like no other man I have ever met before he is sweet and kind he has the most gentle touch ever and he don't want me just for sex and he's not interested in my money he just wants me and it feels good, well Mrs. Taylor you get him but make sure you are careful and don't leap in so fast you know you know u fall in love quickly when you meet someone, I think I've finally learned my lesson Vicki but I promise you I will be careful and wont where my heart on my sleeve anymore it causes too much pain but with frank I will tread lightly and besides he wants to take it slow I've tried so many times to get him to make love to me but he says he's not ready that I should get rid of the bad things in my life and clean it up first that he wants all of me not part of me so I'm working on that and he says he will wait for me, well please be careful anyway I will Vicki thanks as always, you are so welcome, I'm taking off early is there anything I need to know before I leave, no Mrs. Taylor everything's right on schedule, ok I'm going to finish up some things than head out, what if Mr. Nesbit call what would you like for me to do? You can put him through if I'm still here if not he'll call my cell, ok I'm going back to my desk do you need anything? No I'm fine thanks. I started to finish up some work I was excited about going out tonight with frank, I called it a day I wanted to go to the mall and buy a new dress and stop in Victoria secrets to see what new that I want, I went to mall I found a really cute black dress for dancing and a couple more dresses than I went to Victoria secrets they had a new and cute black bra and panty set I wanted to wear with the dress and when I finish in that store I had bought about ten more cute sets maybe one of these will catch frank eyes I headed to sacks to buy me some cute shoes like I don't have enough already but I found a few pair it was time for me to head home, when I got home I made sure the coast was clear and I went in to take me a nice bubble bath all I could do was think about this man and I was getting excited more ways than one, frank had called to say he would pick me up which was fine with me so by the time I got dressed and all pretty up he was down at the front door, I headed to the elevator and went into the lobby I'm usually out the back elevator headed to my car but now I was being picked up at the front door, when I arrived at his car he was standing there with my door open hello frank and greeted him with a kiss, hellllooo denese you look exquisite this evening, thank you frank and you look very good yourself my knight in shining armor, frank had on an Calvin Klein tux he was looking good from head to toe. We arrived at Salvatore's restaurant the ambiance was very elegant frank had made reservations for us we were escorted to our table and it wasn't one in a dark corner either we were in public and he didn't hide me we he ordered us some wine and the restaurant was known for its Italian cuisine and yes lasagna is my favorite so we ordered our salads and our dinner but the conversation was just good and it flowed very well after our meals we decided to dance off some of our food and the first dance was the salsa I loved that dance and frank knew how to dance I had so much fun on the dance floor after a few songs they slowed the music down and frank pulled me into him, denese you look stunning this evening and I'm glad to be here with you, thank you frank I'm glad to be here with you as well we were so close I could feel his groin growing I began to blush, oh frank I see you know how to rise to the occasion we laughed denese you make me rise to the occasion all the time you just didn't know it, by the time the music had stop we were still holding each other not wanting to let go, denese the music has stopped I know frank I just feel so safe in your arms I don't want to let go denese you want have to let go I'm here with you and for you, we headed back to the table frank paid the check and we left we stopped by the marina to look at the boats as we walked down the pier we stopped in front of a boat called "just for you" what a catchy name, it is isn't it we headed to the boat frank whose boat is this, it's mine dense come aboard let me show you around when I stepped inside the cabin there was candles lit all over the place and champagne chilling on ice and rose petals everywhere, frank this is so amazing how did you do this I called my driver and had he to set it up for me the next I knew we were moving I wanted to go on top to the deck to see but it was dark besides the lights from the other yachts and the moonlight it was so beautiful, oh frank this is just amazing but where are we going? Just out to sea for a little bit I hope you don't mind no frank not at all as long as I'm with you he kissed me so passionately in the back of mind I'm thinking yes I wore the right underwear today and began to smile to myself, we headed back down to the cabin area and sat down and had some champagne I was having a hard time resisting this man I wanted to jump his bones but I held my composure, denese are you having a good time yes frank I'm having a lovely time but I didn't know you own a yacht, denese I own a lot of things the only reason I took that job for Mrs. Nesbit is because what happen to my wife other than that I own several high rises in downtown Chicago and other parts of the world when my wife passed I sold the house and just moved into an apartment I was unsure if I was going to be able to go on with my life than I saw you and thought how could someone so beautiful be with an asshoe like that and I desperate to make sure another woman didn't die with this man but after talking to you and sharing I found myself falling for you and realize I needed to get my life back that's why I tell you take your life back you don't need to keep being hurt by this man he is a womanizer and after falling for you I wasn't going to let you be his next victim I know he hits on you and that's about to stop no more of that do you hear me denese yes frank I hear you, denese if you don't love yourself how do you expect a man to love you, you're right frank I don't think I've loved myself in a long time I'm glad we're here together me too denese me too and we started to kiss. Denese I don't think I can contain myself any longer around you, I've tried to be patient but you are just too dam sexy that I'm having a hard time not touching you. Frank please make love to me I really want you too. He began to kiss me again, his lips are so soft and strong, not like Alex in a different way, he began to rub my breast, his hands went behind my back to unzip my dress he took off one shoulder strap and began kissing that shoulder than the other I stood up so my dress could fall to the floor, why denese I like what you're wearing under that dress, I wore it just for you frank he began kissing my neck than back up to my mouth he led me to the bed that was full of rose petals and laid me down gently he climbed on me to continue to kiss me he kissed every inch of my body I could feel myself flaring up on the inside he made his way down to the top of my panties and began to pull them down slowly while kissing my thighs he parted my legs I'm glad I shaved and he began kissing my vagina and his tongue played with my clit oh frank he just kept going I was about to burst frank I'm cumming please stop he just kept going his tongue thrusting in and out of me and he playing with my clit had me squirming all over the bed the next I knew I let go all over him and he was still licking and sucking until I came again and again than he slowly began kissing his way back up to me when he reached my mouth I couldn't wait for him to put his tongue in my mouth and I devoured it he slid himself into me and it felt sooooo good and he we made love he stayed hitting my g-spot and I kept coming frank was all I could scream out of my mouth on that last orgasm we let go together and dam was it good my nipples was so sensitive and he wanted to still play with them frank you need to stop their very sensitive right now I know denese why you think I keep playing with them I know you can't handle it, frank please stop he kept on going so I decided to push him off me and climb on top of him I began kissing him and move down his neck to his sexy chest on to his nipples down his six pack to his penis I sucked his balls before I started with his dick so I could feel him up his dick was like a hard brick by the time I put it in my mouth and I sucked it hard until he came than I climbed back on top of him and put his dick in my hot wet juicy pussy and rode him like the cowgirl I am, oh denese what you trying to do hurt me, oh no frank I don't want to hurt you I'm going to put this pussy on you so good I'm going to be the only person you think about for a while, I fucked him long and hard when I reached my climax we exploded together I wet him up completely, oh frank I can't take no more right now, me either I like the way you squirt though I would eat you just to watch you squirt oh frank you silly I have always been a squirter if you not careful you will be completely soaked by me, its ok it's a good soaking can we please go take a shower, yes denese come on we headed into the shower he didn't forget anything he had my favorite shower gel and lotion I guess he paid attention to what was in my bathroom, I began to wash his body as we stood face to face, denese I wanted to wait to make love to you but you are so irresistible I couldn't wait any longer, frank I'm glad you didn't wait me too he began kissing me under the water than he pushed me up against the shower wall and began to pour body wash over my body and began to lather me up I turned my back to him so he can wash my back he poured the body wash and watched it run down my body his hands reached around to rub my nipples and they stood at attention again I didn't think I had nothing else in me to give but my body says something different he slid himself into me and began to fuck me he thrust me, harder frank harder he went harder, ooooooo give it to me frank give it to me and he gave it to me frank I'm cumming frank ahhhhhhhhh frank once again we came together and lust leaned there against the wall both out of breath frank my legs are so weak I don't think I can move yes you can baby I'll help you he helped me out of the shower he wrapped me up in a town and sat down on the couch I was exhausted so he change the bed linen and I laid down wrapped up in his arm and we went to sleep when the sun was coming up he woke me to come up on deck and watch it oh frank the sunrise is beautiful yes just like you oh frank please I look a hot mess no denese you are beautiful just like this I took the liberty of getting you something to wear to work so there's no need to go home this morning when we dock I will take you ok, yes fine with me he kissed me than I headed back down below to freshen up and get dressed while brushing my teeth he had snuck up behind me hi beautiful hi handsome, I put your clothes on the bed I hope you like them frank so far I've like everything so I'm sure I will like them he thought of everything including panties and bra, how did you know what size to get well I was Victoria secrets and I manage to pay attention to what you were buying, so now you're spying on me no not like that all I want to make sure you're safe that's all, is that the truth yes denese I know how dangerous Alex is and since he has not seen you lately I know he's looking for you so I want to keep you safe until he's locked up is that alright with you, yes its fine with me I like having your sexy ass following me, we laughed it was a really nice skirt and jacket and the bra and panties was perfect, thank you frank its gorgeous and it fits perfectly, glad you like it now you show the world they can't keep your head down go strut your stuff we docked and walked up the pier to the car frank drove me to work and kissed me as I got out the car when I walked through the door I could feel someone watching me and I knew it wasn't frank so I went on into my office and closed the door Vicki walked in and startled me, hello there Mrs. Taylor are you ok, yes Vicki I'm fine, than my cell phone ranged hello, denese don't be scared I saw Alex watching you and I know you felt it but baby its ok I'll be right here with you so calm down and don't worry, frank how did you know, denese you looked frantic when you exited the car I knew who it was that scared you, thank you frank you are a life saver I'm meeting with my husband this afternoon when I get off work ok I'll keep my eyes on Alex you go handle your business and I will check on you soon ok goodbye. Mrs. Taylor are you sure alright? I am now Vicki thanks for asking, well here is your morning coffee and your messages and the contractors are here in the conference room, ok I'll be there shortly make sure they have coffee, I did they have coffee and doughnuts, they are good, ok I'll right there. After my meeting and learning everything was on schedule I was happy about it. I made a few more calls and got ready to leave so I called my husband and asked him where did he want to meet he asked if I would come by the house I said yes no problem I went to my office bathroom to freshen up my make-up and hair I wanted to look extra good to let him know what he's missed out on. I called frank to tell him I was heading out, ok be careful baby and call me when you're done with your meeting if you're up to it, ok I will and thanks frank for everything, you are so welcome baby I will be here if you need me, ok bye. I arrived at the house, my husband let me in hello Charles, hello denese come on in, you look really good, thank you, what did you want to see me about Charles, dam denese you look good how have you been, thank you and I've been fine, now what do you want to see me about, I wanted to see how you were doing and I can see you're doing good, you thought I wouldn't you thought after you hurt me the way you did that I would still be depressed and crying every day and looking ugly, instead of this fabulous, what you thought was that you broke me completely and I will never recover from you but you are wrong as a matter of fact I've contacted my attorney and had the papers drawn up for our divorce, so what did you want to see me about Charles I have a meeting, denese I want to apologize to you for really hurting you the way I did, denese I didn't really know what I had until you left me I've been miserable without you and I want you to come home come back to me. Charles do you have any idea what you did to me you slept with my best friend in my bed you were seeing her for a while you slept with other people I've known, you would lie about your whereabouts you were always someplace you shouldn't have been you treated me like a kid and sometimes like your roommate and not your wife, you use to take your car keys to the other car so I couldn't go anywhere while you were off fucking somebody else. I would clean up the house and go to class while you were here fucking somebody in my bed, you would go to the hotels with whomever, denese, no I'm going to get this off my chest I lost my job and you wouldn't help me keep none of my stuff all you cared about was your things you wanted now I'm able to buy anything in the world I want without help from anybody, you never had time to be with me you wanted to be with other people since I wouldn't give you a threesome you decided to have your own, you spent more time on the computer looking at pussy than you did looking at mine, we hadn't slept together in years and that was your fault you wanted someone else I guess to do what you were used to getting at the strip clubs or you wanted someone who was much smaller than me I don't know what your reasons were but you hurt me bad now I have moved on after months of crying and trying to figure out what had I done so bad to be treated so horribly I cried for months trying to figure this out I tried to kill myself I gained so much weight Charles I felt like nothing like less than garbage and you did that to me, but now look at me I'm one of the wealthiest people around I own several companies I lost weight I look good I feel good and I'm happy, happier than I have been in a very long time Charles I am good but you know what I can't fully move on with my life until I ask you to forgive me and I forgive you, Charles can you please forgive me for everything I have ever done to you, yes denese but I need you to forgive me I'm so sorry that I hurt you like that I didn't know what I had done to you I'm really sorry, mark I forgive you and I will always love you because you are the father of my children and I will always be your friend but for me that's as far as it goes, Charles I do thank you cause we did have some good years together and we had some beautiful children that we raised up to be great. All our time together wasn't bad just the past ten years or so were not good for me, so now I'm fine and I'm good so there is nothing to fight over so when the papers come just signed them and turn them in I'm not going to argue about the house you can do whatever you want to do with the house and keep your cars I'm not asking for anything you can have it all, denese I hope you don't hate me, no Charles not any more, like I said I'm sorry and I do forgive you but can I say one thing to you, yes Charles what is it, you look happy and you look dam good whatever you doing keep it up I hope one day maybe we can get back together, Charles we will always be here for each other that much I'm sure of and who knows what the future holds for us we have to wait and see, well don't get mad when I try to win you back, ok Charles I have to go, can I have a kiss for the road, sure I kissed him on his cheek, wow on the cheek I'm not sure where your lips been these days, trust me they haven't been on anybody, well a lady can never be too sure bye Charles talk to later, bye denese thanks for coming by and I'm glad we got a chance to talk and you were able to vent all your anger that I caused and once again I am truly sorry for all the hurt and pain that I have caused you, it was nice to finally get it out to you and I really feel better, I walked out got into my car and left I called frank on my way home, hi frank, hi denese how did it go, it actually went well I'm glad I went and got that one over with so now I'm on my way home are you coming over tonight? Maybe later I have some things to finish up first, ok call me I'm going to make me some tuna salad and watch some TV tonight, ok babe I will call you later.

CHAPTER 21

I arrived home and not paying attention to see if Alex was there or not I pulled into my parking spot got on the elevator and went up by the time I closed my door there was a pounding on my door who is it? Open the dam door before I break it down Alex what the hell is wrong with you now? You think you can go all over town with another man and I wouldn't notice(slap) I've had enough of you putting your dam hands on me, you nothing but a dam whoe, Alex get the fuck out of my house now, oh no I'm going to show you about being out here with another man when I get through with you he's not going to want you, he pushed me into the wall you running around here cheating on your wife you got a lot of nerve (punch) you say what now he punched me in my face than in my stomach I fought back and got a loose and ran to my room, he grabbed my legs come back here bitch he continued to beat on me I got away I manage to reached my gun, oh you gone shoot me, you womanizing mother fucker you will not hit me ever again, you run around here fucking with married women and beat them and one you even cause to kill herself but not me I'm taking my life back and ending you he leaped at me I shot him in the arm, I heard frank and the police kick my door in, denese stop if you kill him you're going to jail right now it's just self-defense, no frank he will not get another chance to hurt another woman, who is this you knight and shining armor, this the man I saw you with, yes it is he's also the man of the woman you use to beat and caused her to kill herself, oh now I remember you, you came into my hotel room when I was putting that bitch of yours in her place, not my fault your wife was in love with this dick and she didn't know how to handle it, frank jumped on him and started punching him in his face, frank stop shouted detective Mendoza, Alex's wife walked in, you see the monster you created you knew what he was doing and you should have turned in a long time ago Mrs. Nesbit, I'm sorry Mrs. Taylor now he can go to jail, for what first of all for putting your hands on me, second of all for driving this man's wife to kill herself, you drove her into killing herself, you took away her life now I'm going to take away yours. You use to beat her too but I'm going to make sure you rot in prison and if you ever get out and come near me again I swear to you Alex I will kill you now get that piece of trash out my house. Frank took me the emergency room to be checked out, I had three broken ribs and a broken jaw bone and some bruises and a split lip, I will never tell my family about this frank this, after my hospital visit frank took me home they already had my locks and my alarm code changed, I also change my parking space in the garage. I laid on the couch, frank I'm sorry I wasn't more careful, denese it's not your fault Alex has had woman issues since he was a teenager now he's finally going to jail and maybe some counseling or anger management class, frank I don't want to talk about him I just want to shower and lay in my bed, come on I will wash you up as frank began to take my clothes off I was looking in the mirror and started to cry the tears were just falling frank didn't say anything just let me cry he helped me in the shower my felt like I was hit by a truck it was so sore he washed me and then dried me off he took me to my bedroom and put my nightie on me and laid me in the bed I was still crying, denese I'll be right back with some water and your pain pills, he came back I took two pills and laid back down frank laid with me, denese you're going to be alright I will make sure of that so you can cry all you want and when you're ready to talk I'll be here for you now close your eyes and go to sleep. A few months have passed and me and frank were dating and taking things slowly when I got a letter in the mail that Alex took a plea deal on the assault with intent to commit murder, he only got 5-15 years which means he will be out in 5 years how the hell did that happen Alex had the best lawyers his wife's money could buy and yes she paid the attorneys to defend that sick bastard.